FOR WHOM THE BELL TOLLS

Ernest Hemingway

EDITORIAL DIRECTOR Justin Kestler
EXECUTIVE EDITOR Ben Florman
DIRECTOR OF TECHNOLOGY Tammy Hepps

SERIES EDITORS John Crowther, Justin Kestler
MANAGING EDITOR Vince Janoski

WRITER Anna Medvedovsky
EDITOR Matt Blanchard

Copyright © 2003 by SparkNotes LLC

All rights reserved. No part of this book may be used or reproduced in any manner whatsoever without the written permission of the Publisher.

SPARKNOTES is a registered trademark of SparkNotes LLC

This edition published by Spark Publishing

Spark Publishing
A Division of SparkNotes LLC
120 Fifth Avenue, 8th Floor
New York, NY 10011

Any book purchased without a cover is stolen property, reported as "unsold and destroyed" to the Publisher, who receives no payment for such "stripped books."

First edition.

Please submit all comments and questions or report errors to www.sparknotes.com/errors

Library of Congress Catalog-in-Publication Data available upon request

Printed and bound in the United States

ISBN 1-58663-830-0

Introduction: Stopping to Buy SparkNotes on a Snowy Evening

Whose words these are you *think* you know.
Your paper's due tomorrow, though;
We're glad to see you stopping here
To get some help before you go.

Lost your course? You'll find it here.
Face tests and essays without fear.
Between the words, good grades at stake:
Get great results throughout the year.

Once school bells caused your heart to quake
As teachers circled each mistake.
Use SparkNotes and no longer weep,
Ace every single test you take.

Yes, books are lovely, dark, and deep,
But only what you grasp you keep,
With hours to go before you sleep,
With hours to go before you sleep.

Contents

CONTEXT	1
PLOT OVERVIEW	5
CHARACTER LIST	9
ANALYSIS OF MAJOR CHARACTERS	15
ROBERT JORDAN	15
PABLO	16
PILAR	17
MARIA	17
THEMES, MOTIFS & SYMBOLS	19
THE LOSS OF INNOCENCE IN WAR	19
THE VALUE OF HUMAN LIFE	19
ROMANTIC LOVE AS SALVATION	20
RABBITS AND HARES	21
THE FOREST FLOOR	21
SIGNS AND OMENS	22
SUICIDE	22
PLANES, TANKS, AND MORTARS	23
ABSINTHE	23
SUMMARY & ANALYSIS	25
EPIGRAPH AND CHAPTERS ONE–TWO	25
CHAPTERS THREE–SEVEN	28
CHAPTERS EIGHT–THIRTEEN	31
CHAPTERS FOURTEEN–SEVENTEEN	36
CHAPTERS EIGHTEEN–TWENTY	39
CHAPTERS TWENTY-ONE–TWENTY-SIX	42
CHAPTERS TWENTY-SEVEN–TWENTY-NINE	45
CHAPTERS THIRTY–THIRTY-THREE	47
CHAPTERS THIRTY-FOUR–THIRTY-NINE	50
CHAPTERS FORTY–FORTY-TWO	53
CHAPTER FORTY-THREE	56

IMPORTANT QUOTATIONS EXPLAINED	59
KEY FACTS	65
STUDY QUESTIONS & ESSAY TOPICS	69
STUDY QUESTIONS	69
SUGGESTED ESSAY TOPICS	73
REVIEW & RESOURCES	75
QUIZ	75
SUGGESTIONS FOR FURTHER READING	81

Context

ERNEST HEMINGWAY WAS BORN IN 1899 in a wealthy, conservative Chicago suburb. The second of six children, he showed an early talent in writing that he honed through work on his high school's literary magazine and student newspaper. Upon graduating from high school in 1917, Hemingway moved away from home and embarked on a professional writing career, starting as a reporter for the *Kansas City Star*.

In 1918, during the height of World War I, Hemingway volunteered to serve as an ambulance driver for the Red Cross, which sent him to Italy. Within just a few weeks of his arrival, Hemingway was injured by an exploding shell and was sent to a hospital in Milan. During his recovery, he became romantically involved with a nurse—an episode that he portrayed years later in his novel *A Farewell to Arms* (1929).

After the war, Hemingway worked as a newspaper correspondent in Paris, where he moved among a circle of expatriate artists and writers, including American writers F. Scott Fitzgerald and Gertrude Stein, Irish writer James Joyce, and Spanish painter Pablo Picasso. Stein, in particular, became Hemingway's mentor. Some critics have suggested that she provided the inspiration for the character Pilar in *For Whom the Bell Tolls*, who serves as a mother figure for the protagonist, Robert Jordan.

During his time as a correspondent, Hemingway traveled extensively in Spain and developed a strong interest in Spanish culture. He became especially interested in bullfighting, which he viewed as a uniquely Spanish experience that accustomed Spaniards to face death and thus enabled them to live fuller lives. Hemingway's interest in Spain led to literary masterpieces such as *The Sun Also Rises* (1926), a chronicle of a group of disaffected Americans in postwar France and Spain, and *Death in the Afternoon* (1932), a nonfiction work about bullfighting.

For Whom the Bell Tolls (1940) takes place during the Spanish Civil War, which ravaged the country throughout the late 1930s. Tensions in Spain began to rise as early as 1931, when a group of left-wing Republicans overthrew the country's monarchy in a bloodless coup. The new Republican government then proposed controversial religious reforms that angered right-wing Fascists, who had the support of the army and the Catholic church.

After a strong Communist turnout in the 1936 popular elections, the Fascist army commander Generalísimo Francisco Franco initiated a coup in an attempt to overthrow the Republican government. Unexpectedly, the key cities of Madrid and Barcelona remained loyal to the Republic. This divide marked the beginning of the Spanish Civil War, a conflict between the right-wing Fascists (Nationalists) and the left-wing Republicans (Loyalists), a large number of whom were Communists. Violence exploded all over Spain, and both sides committed atrocities. Many western countries saw the Spanish Civil War as a symbolic struggle between fascism and democracy. Eventually, the superior military machine of the Fascist alliance prevailed, and the war ended in the spring of 1939.

During the Spanish Civil War, Hemingway was involved in the production of two Loyalist propaganda documentary films. Later in the conflict, he served as a war correspondent for the North American Newspaper Alliance. *For Whom the Bell Tolls* expresses Hemingway's strong feelings about the war, both a critique of the Republicans' leadership and a lament over the Fascists' destruction of the earthy way of life of the Spanish peasantry. The novel is set in the spring of 1937, at a time when the war had come to a standstill, a month after German troops razed the Spanish town of Guernica. At this point, the Republicans still held out some hope for victory and were planning a new offensive. *For Whom the Bell Tolls* explores themes of wartime individuality, the effects of war on its combatants, and the military bureaucracy's impersonal indifference to human life. Most important, the novel addresses the question of whether an idealistic view of the world justifies violence.

Hemingway's novels are known for portraying a particular type of hero. Critic Philip Young famously termed this figure a "code hero," a man who gracefully struggles against death and obliteration. Robert Jordan, the protagonist of *For Whom the Bell Tolls*, is a prime example of this kind of hero. The tragedy of the code hero is that he is mortal and knows that he will ultimately lose the struggle. Meanwhile, he lives according to a code—hence the term code hero—that helps him endure a life full of stress and tension with courage and grace. He appreciates the physical pleasures of this world—food, drink, sex, and so on—without obsessing over them.

Hemingway is particularly known for his journalistic prose style, which was revolutionary at the time and has influenced countless writers since. Hemingway's writing is succinct and direct, although his speakers tend to give the impression that they are leaving a tremendous amount unsaid. This bold experimentation with prose earned Hemingway the 1953 Pulitzer Prize and 1954 Nobel Prize for Literature for his most popular work, the novella *The Old Man and the Sea* (1952).

Although Hemingway wrote several more novels afterward, he was never again able to match the success of *The Old Man and the Sea*. In the late 1950s, the combination of depression, deteriorating health, and frustration with his writing began to weigh heavily on him. His depression worsened, and in July 1961, he died of a self-inflicted gunshot wound in Ketchum, Idaho. Although Hemingway's long career ended sadly, his novels and short stories remain as popular today as ever before, and he maintains a reputation as one of the most innovative and influential authors of the twentieth century.

Plot Overview

For whom the bell tolls opens in May 1937, at the height of the Spanish Civil War. An American man named Robert Jordan, who has left the United States to enlist on the Republican side in the war, travels behind enemy lines to work with Spanish guerrilla fighters, or *guerrilleros*, hiding in the mountains. The Republican command has assigned Robert Jordan the dangerous and difficult task of blowing up a Fascist-controlled bridge as part of a larger Republican offensive.

A peasant named Anselmo guides Robert Jordan to the guerrilla camp, which is hidden in a cave. Along the way, they encounter Pablo, the leader of the camp, who greets Robert Jordan with hostility and opposes the bridge operation because he believes it endangers the *guerrilleros*' safety. Robert Jordan suspects that Pablo may betray or sabotage the mission.

At the camp, Robert Jordan meets Pilar, Pablo's "woman." A large, sturdy part-gypsy, Pilar appears to be the real leader of the band of *guerrilleros*. A rapport quickly develops between Robert Jordan and Pilar. During the course of the evening, Robert Jordan meets the six other inhabitants of the camp: the unreliable Rafael, feisty and foul-mouthed Agustín, dignified Fernando, old Primitivo, and brothers Andrés and Eladio. The camp also shelters a young woman named Maria, whom a band of Fascists raped not long before. Robert Jordan and Maria are immediately drawn to each other.

Robert Jordan and Anselmo leave the camp to scout out the bridge. When they return, Pablo publicly announces that neither he nor his *guerrilleros* will help blow up the bridge. Pilar and the others disagree, however, so Pablo sullenly gives in. Privately, Rafael urges Robert Jordan to kill Pablo, but Pilar insists that Pablo is not dangerous. That night, Maria comes out to join Robert Jordan as he sleeps outside. They profess love for each other and make love.

The next morning, Pilar leads Robert Jordan through the forest to consult with El Sordo, the leader of another band of *guerrilleros*, about the bridge operation. They take Maria along. El Sordo agrees to help with the mission, but both he and Robert Jordan are troubled by the fact that the bridge must be blown in daylight, which will make their retreat more difficult. On the way back to Pablo's camp, Robert Jordan and Maria make love in the forest. When they catch up with Pilar, Maria confesses to Pilar that the earth moved as they made love. Pilar, impressed, says that such a thing happens no more than three times in a person's lifetime.

Back at the camp, a drunken Pablo insults Robert Jordan, who tries to provoke Pablo, hoping to find an excuse to kill him. Pablo refuses to be provoked, even when Agustín hits him in the face. When Pablo steps away for a few minutes, the others agree that he is dangerous and must be killed. Robert Jordan volunteers to do it. Suddenly, Pablo returns and announces that he has changed his mind and will help with the bridge. Later that night, Maria comes outside to sleep with Robert Jordan again. They talk about their feeling that they are one person, that they share the same body.

In the morning, Robert Jordan wakes up, sees a Fascist cavalryman, and shoots him, awakening the camp. After breakfast, the group hears sounds of a fight in the distance, and Robert Jordan believes that the Fascists are attacking El Sordo's camp. Agustín and Primitivo want to aid El Sordo, but Robert Jordan and Pilar know that it likely would be useless.

The scene shifts to El Sordo's hill, which a group of Fascists is assaulting. El Sordo's men play dead and manage to shoot the Fascist captain, but several minutes later, Fascist planes bomb the hilltop and kill everyone in El Sordo's band. The ranking Fascist officer orders the beheading of all the corpses of El Sordo's men.

The *guerrilleros* at Pablo's camp, having heard the planes bomb El Sordo's hill, feel glum as they eat lunch. Robert Jordan writes a dispatch to the Republican command recommending that both the bridge operation and the larger offensive be canceled, for the Fascists are aware of the plan and the operation will not succeed. He sends Andrés to deliver the dispatch to the headquarters of General Golz, a Republican leader. Maria again joins Robert Jordan in his sleeping bag that night, and they fantasize about their future life in Madrid.

Meanwhile, in Madrid, Robert Jordan's friend, a Russian journalist named Karkov, learns that the Fascists know about the offensive the Republicans have planned for the next day. Karkov worries about Robert Jordan.

At two in the morning, Pilar wakes Robert Jordan and reports that Pablo has fled the camp with some of the explosives that were meant to blow the bridge. Though furious at first, Robert Jordan controls his anger and plans to carry out the operation anyway, with fewer explosives. He wakes up Maria, and as they make love, they feel the earth move again. Pablo suddenly returns just before dawn, claiming that he left in a moment of weakness. He says that he threw the explosives into the river but felt great loneliness after doing so. He has brought back five men with their horses from neighboring guerrilla bands to help. The fighters take their positions.

The scene shifts to Andrés, who has been traveling through the night to deliver Robert Jordan's dispatch to General Golz. Crossing into Republican territory, Andrés is slowed when several suspicious but apathetic officers question him. When Andrés and his escort finally near Golz's headquarters, a politician named André Marty suspects that they are Fascist spies and orders them arrested. Robert Jordan's friend Karkov hears about the arrests and uses his influence to free the men. Robert Jordan's dispatch finally reaches Golz but arrives too late. The Republican offensive already has begun and can no longer be stopped.

As dawn breaks, Robert Jordan and Anselmo descend on the bridge, shoot the Fascist sentries, and plant the explosives. Pilar arrives and says that Eladio has been killed, while Fernando, fatally wounded, must be left behind. When Robert Jordan detonates the explosives, the bridge falls, but shrapnel from the blast strikes Anselmo and kills him. Pablo emerges from below, saying that all five of his men are dead. Agustín accuses Pablo of shooting the men for their horses, and Pablo does not deny it.

As the group crosses the road in retreat, a Fascist bullet hits Robert Jordan's horse, which tramples on Robert Jordan's left leg, breaking it. Knowing that he must be left behind, Robert Jordan says goodbye to Maria, saying that he will be with her even if she goes. Pilar and Pablo lead Maria away.

Alone, Robert Jordan contemplates suicide but resolves to stay alive to hold off the Fascists. He is grateful for having lived, in his final few days, a full lifetime. For the first time, he feels "integrated," in harmony with the world. As the Fascist lieutenant approaches, Robert Jordan takes aim, feeling his heart beating against the floor of the forest.

Character List

Robert Jordan An American volunteer for the Republican side in the Spanish Civil War and the protagonist of *For Whom the Bell Tolls*. Robert Jordan is pragmatic, very good at what he does, and never lets his emotions interfere with his work. He appreciates physical pleasures like smelling pine trees, drinking absinthe, and having sex. At the same time, he is conflicted about his role within the war and within the larger world. Interior dialogues in which he argues with himself about these conflicts constitute a significant part of the novel. Over the course of the novel, he gradually resolves these tensions and learns to integrate his rational, thinking side with his intuitive, feeling side.

Pablo The leader of the guerrilla camp. Pablo is an individualist who feels responsible only to himself. Hemingway often compares him to a bull, a boar, and other burly, stubborn, and unpleasant animals. Pablo used to be a great fighter and a great man but has now started drinking and has "gone bad," as many characters remark. Tired of the war and attached to his horses, Pablo is ready to betray the Republican cause at the start of the novel.

Pilar Pablo's part-gypsy "woman." Pilar means "pillar" in Spanish, and indeed, the fiercely patriotic, stocky, and steadfast Pilar is—if not the absolute leader—the support center of the guerrilla group. Pilar keeps the hearth, fights in battle, mothers Robert Jordan, and bullies Pablo and Rafael. She has an intuitive, mystical connection to deeper truths about the working of the world.

Maria — A young woman with Pablo's band who falls in love with Robert Jordan. The victim of rape at the hands of Fascists who took over her town, Maria is frequently described by means of earth imagery. Hemingway compares her movements to a colt's, and Robert Jordan affectionately calls her "Rabbit."

Anselmo — An old, trustworthy guerrilla fighter. For Robert Jordan, Anselmo represents all that is good about Spaniards. He lives close to the land, is loyal, follows directions, and stays where he is told. He likes to hunt but has not developed a taste for the kill and hates killing people. Anselmo has stopped praying ever since the Communists banned organized religion but admits that he misses it.

Agustín — A trustworthy and high-spirited guerrilla fighter. Agustín, who mans the machine gun, curses frequently and is secretly in love with Maria.

Fernando — A guerrilla fighter in his mid-thirties. Short and with a lazy eye, Fernando is dignified and literal-minded, embraces bureaucracy, and is easily offended by vulgarities. These factors, combined with his lack of a sense of humor, make Fernando the frequent target of Pilar's jokes.

Primitivo — An elderly guerrilla fighter. Despite his gray hair and broken nose, Primitivo has not learned the cynicism needed for survival in the war. His name, which means "primitive," evokes his idealism as well as the basic, earthy lifestyle of all the *guerrilleros*.

Rafael — A gypsy member of the guerrilla band. Frequently described as well-meaning but "worthless," Rafael proves his worthlessness by leaving his lookout post at a crucial moment. He is a foil for the trustworthy Anselmo, who does not leave his post on the previous night despite the cold and the snow. Rafael has few loyalties and does not believe in political causes.

Andrés   One of the guerrilla fighters, in his late twenties. Andrés comes into conflict with the Republican leaders' bureaucracy in his attempt to deliver Robert Jordan's dispatch to the Republican command. Andrés serves also a foil to Pablo: although both Andrés and Pablo enjoy killing in an almost sexual way, Andrés has had the opportunity to satisfy that thirst through his experience with bull-baiting during a town fiesta. As a result, unlike Pablo, Andrés has learned to identify and control his desire to kill.

Eladio   Andrés's older brother and another of the guerrilla fighters. The jumpy Eladio plays a relatively minor role in the novel. His most noticeable feature is that Robert Jordan repeatedly forgets his name. His death at the end of the novel attracts little notice.

El Sordo (Santiago)   The leader of a guerrilla band that operates near Pablo's. Short, heavy, and gray-haired, El Sordo (Spanish for "the deaf one") is a man of few words. Like Robert Jordan, he is excited by a successful kill and is sad to die.

Joaquín   One of the members of El Sordo's band. Joaquín originally wanted to be bullfighter but was too scared. He lost most of his family at the hands of the Fascists and cries when he talks about them. Joaquín buys into the Republicans' propaganda but turns back to religion at the moment of his death, illustrating the emptiness of political rhetoric in times of true crisis.

General Golz   The Russian general, allied with the Republicans, who assigns Robert Jordan the bridge-blowing mission. Robert Jordan says that Golz is the best general he has served under, but the Republican military bureaucracy impedes all of Golz's operations. Golz believes that thinking is useless because it breaks down resolve and impedes action.

Kashkin — A Russian guerrilla operative who once worked with Pablo's band to blow up a train. Although Kashkin never appears in the novel, he is a foil for Robert Jordan. Unlike Robert Jordan, Kashkin was openly nervous.

Karkov — A well-connected foreign correspondent for the Russian newspaper Pravda and Robert Jordan's friend in Madrid. Karkov, the most intelligent man Robert Jordan knows, teaches Robert Jordan about the harsh realities of wartime politics. Karkov believes that abstract philosophy is superior to action and intuition.

Captain Rogelio Gomez — A former barber and now commander of the battalion that Andrés first reaches after crossing the Republican lines. Gomez romanticizes the idea of guerrilla warfare and escorts Andrés to several commanders, trying to reach General Golz.

Lieutenant-Colonel Miranda — A Republican staff office brigade commander. Miranda's only goal in the war is not to be demoted from his current rank. He is one of many examples of apathetic or inept Republican commanders who contribute to the eventual Republican defeat.

André Marty — The French Commissar of the International Brigades, the troops of foreign volunteers who serve on the Republican side in the war. Marty has become blinded by political paranoia and is convinced that he is surrounded by enemies.

Lieutenant Paco Berrendo — A devoutly Catholic Fascist officer who orders the beheading of El Sordo's men. Berrendo's sorrow for his dead friend, his awareness of the useless horror of war, and his tendency toward introspection make him a sympathetic character. Hemingway's portrayal of Berrendo underscores the fact that the enemy side is not faceless but composed of real individuals who also make real and difficult decisions.

Captain Moro An overconfident Fascist commander in charge of taking El Sordo's hill. Moro serves as a foil for the more introspective Lieutenant Berrendo.

Finito de Palencia Pilar's former lover, a bullfighter who died from complications from wounds received in a bullfight. Short, sad-eyed, and sullen, Finito was brave in the ring in spite of his fear of bulls. Finito, who appears in the novel only in Pilar's flashbacks, exemplifies the courage of Hemingway's code hero and Hemingway's deep respect for the bullfighting profession.

Robert Jordan's father A weak, religious man who could not stand up to his aggressive wife and eventually committed suicide. His father's weakness is a constant source of embarrassment to Robert Jordan.

Robert Jordan's grandfather A veteran of the American Civil War and a member of the Republican National Committee. Robert Jordan feels more closely related to his grandfather than to his father.

Analysis of Major Characters

Robert Jordan

The protagonist of *For Whom the Bell Tolls*, Robert Jordan left his job as a college instructor in the United States to volunteer for the Republican side in the Spanish Civil War. Initially, he believed in the Republican cause with a near-religious faith and felt an "absolute brotherhood" with his comrades on the Republican side. However, when the action of the novel starts, we see that Robert Jordan has become disillusioned. As the conflict drags on, he realizes that he does not really believe in the Republican cause but joined their side simply because they fought against Fascism. Because he fights for a side whose causes he does not necessarily support, Robert Jordan experiences a great deal of internal conflict and begins to wonder whether there is really any difference between the Fascist and Republican sides.

Robert Jordan's interior monologues and actions indicate these internal conflicts that plague him. Although he is disillusioned with the Republican cause, he continues to fight for that cause. In public he announces that he is anti-Fascist rather than a Communist, but in private he thinks that he has no politics at all. He knows that his job requires that he kill people but also knows that he should not believe in killing in the abstract. Despite his newfound love for Maria, he feels that there cannot be a place for her in his life while he also has his military work. He claims not to be superstitious but cannot stop thinking about the world as giving him signs of things to come. These conflicts weigh heavily on Robert Jordan throughout the bulk of the novel.

Robert Jordan resolves these tensions at the end of *For Whom the Bell Tolls*, in his final moments as he faces death. He accepts himself as a man of action rather than thought, as a man who believes in practicality rather than abstract theories. He understands that the war requires him to do some things that he does not believe in. He also realizes that, though he cannot forget the unsavory deeds he has done in the past, he must avoid dwelling on them for the sake of getting things done in the present. Ultimately, Robert Jordan is able to make room in his mind for both his love for Maria and his military mission. By the end of the novel, just before he dies, his internal conflicts and tensions are resolved and he feels "integrated" into the world.

Pablo

Pablo, the exasperating leader of the guerrilla band, is a complex character and an unpredictable force in the novel—a man who is difficult to like but ultimately difficult to condemn unwaveringly. Pablo and Robert Jordan view each other with mutual suspicion and dislike from the start: Pablo adamantly opposes the bridge operation and views Robert Jordan as a threat to the *guerrilleros*' safety, while Robert Jordan senses that Pablo will betray the *guerrilleros* and sabotage the mission. Hemingway uses a variety of unflattering imagery to highlight Pablo's uncooperative and confrontational nature, often comparing Pablo to a bull, a boar, and other stubborn and unpleasant animals.

In virtually all of his actions, Pablo displays a selfish lack of restraint, an irresponsible individualism that contrasts with Robert Jordan's pragmatic and morally motivated outlook. Pablo rashly follows his impulses, whether in the cruel slaughter of the Fascists in his hometown or in the theft of Robert Jordan's explosives. Although this self-indulgence made Pablo a strong and courageous fighter when he was younger, it now proves a liability, for it sows dissent within the guerrilla band and jeopardizes the mission. As Pilar says, Pablo once would have sacrificed anything for the Republican cause but has "gone bad" as the war has dragged on and now wavers in his loyalties.

Despite Pablo's disagreeable characteristics, however, he is not an evil man, and we cannot label him a villain. Although he is stubborn, rash, and sometimes brutal, Pablo displays a clear sense of conscience and realizes when he has done something wrong. He wishes he could bring back to life the Fascists he massacred in his town, and he characterizes his theft of Robert Jordan's explosives as a "moment of weakness." At the same time, however, it is impossible to ignore the fact that Pablo feels remorse over a deed only after it's too late to do anything about it. Above all, Pablo fears death and is exhausted with the war. He simply wants the war to end so that he may live a peaceful life in the country along with Pilar and his horses—a sentiment that is difficult to judge harshly. Ironically, it is

Pablo, not Robert Jordan, who survives at the end of the novel. However, although Pablo stays alive, he does so without the moral strength that Robert Jordan maintains and develops throughout *For Whom the Bell Tolls*.

PILAR

Arguably the most colorful and likable character in *For Whom the Bell Tolls*, Pilar embodies the earthiness, strength, and wisdom of the Spanish peasantry. A large, robust, part-gypsy woman, Pilar exercises great influence over the band of *guerrilleros*—in fact, we quickly become aware that Pablo leads the band in name only. The strong and stable Pilar provides the motivating force behind many of the novel's events. She pushes Robert Jordan and Maria's romance, commands the allegiance of the guerrilla fighters, and organizes the *guerrilleros*' brief alliance with El Sordo. She acts as the support structure for the camp as she unites the band of guerrilla fighters into a family, cooks for all, and sews Robert Jordan's packs. In short, Pilar manipulates the most important characters in *For Whom the Bell Tolls* and sets in place many of the encounters that drive the plot.

Pilar, though practical, often relies on intuitive, mystical, gypsy folk wisdom. Shrewd and worldly-wise, she claims a deep connection to the primitive forces of fate. She claims to be able to smell death, and she describes the smell in repulsively naturalistic detail. She reads palms and interprets sexual experiences. Despite Robert Jordan's cynicism, Pilar's predictions do come true. Pilar exhibits the inevitable sadness that comes with knowledge: "Neither bull force nor bull courage lasted, she knew now, and what did last? I last. . . . But for what?" In the end, the only aspect of Pilar's personality that seems not to show wisdom is her unswerving commitment to and belief in the Republican side, which ultimately loses the war.

MARIA

The young, gentle Maria catches Robert Jordan's eye from the moment he meets her. She exudes a natural, glowing beauty, despite the fact that she has recently suffered a traumatic rape and has had most of her hair shorn off. Though she is vulnerable and lays her emotions bare, she exhibits an inner strength, determination, and resilience that enable her to bear her difficult circumstances. Some critics contend that Hemingway intends Maria to represent the land of Spain itself, ravaged by the warring forces beyond her comprehension, yet always enduring, beautiful, and loving. Indeed, Hemingway frequently uses earth imagery to describe Maria, comparing her hair to the "golden brown of a grain field" and her breasts to "small hills." In this light, Robert Jordan's closeness with Maria mirrors his closeness with Spain, his adopted country.

As Robert Jordan's love interest, Maria provides the impetus for his personal development from an unfeeling thinker and doer to a romantic individual. In his conversations with General Golz and with Maria early in the novel, Robert Jordan reveals his belief that he does not have time for women during the war. Even after Robert meets Maria, he remains closed to extreme emotion or romance. Though in love with her, Robert Jordan still shuts her out whenever he must think about his work. However, by the end of the novel, Robert Jordan thanks Maria for everything that she has taught him and faces the day of his mission noting that he has integrated his commitments to work and to love. Maria, determined to embrace their love fully, teaches Robert Jordan how to resolve his tensions between love and work.

Some critics of *For Whom the Bell Tolls* consider Maria a weak link in the novel because her characterization depends so heavily on the effect she has on Robert Jordan rather than on her own motivations and conflicts. These critics argue that Maria's submissiveness and the speed with which her affair with Robert Jordan progresses are unrealistic. They assert that Maria is not a believable character but rather a stereotype or the embodiment of a male fantasy. Some feminist critics have blanched at Hemingway's treatment of Maria's rape, especially at the fact that sexual intercourse with Robert Jordan appears to heal Maria instantaneously. But although Maria does come across as a rather static character, this flatness renders her symbolic importance all the more apparent. Maria's lovely image endures beyond the last pages of the novel, an emblem of a land that maintains its beauty, strength, and dignity in the face of forces that threaten to tear it apart.

Themes, Motifs & Symbols

Themes

Themes are the fundamental and often universal ideas explored in a literary work.

The Loss of Innocence in War

Each of the characters in *For Whom the Bell Tolls* loses his or her psychological or physical innocence to the war. Some endure tangible traumas: Joaquín loses both his parents and is forced to grow up quickly, while Maria loses her physical innocence when she is raped by a group of Fascist soldiers. On top of these tangible, physical costs of the war come many psychological costs. Robert Jordan initially came to Spain with idealism about the Republican cause and believed confidently that he was joining the good side. But after fighting in the war, Robert Jordan becomes cynical about the Republican cause and loses much of his initial idealism.

The victims of violence in the war are not the only ones to lose their innocence—the perpetrators lose their innocence too. The ruffians in Pablo's hometown who participate in the massacre of the town Fascists have to face their inner brutality afterward. Anselmo has to suppress his aversion to killing human beings, and Lieutenant Berrendo has to quell his aversion to cutting heads off of corpses.

War even costs the innocence of people who aren't involved in it directly. War journalists, writers, and we as readers of novels like *For Whom the Bell Tolls* have to abandon our innocent expectation that wars involve clean moral choices that distinguish us from the enemy. Hemingway shows in the novel that morality is subjective and conditional, and that the sides of right and wrong are almost never clear-cut. With no definite sides of right and wrong in *For Whom the Bell Tolls*, there is no sense of glorious victory in battle, no sense of triumph or satisfaction that good prevails and evil is defeated.

The Value of Human Life

Many characters die during the course of the novel, and we see characters repeatedly question what can possibly justify killing another human being. Anselmo and Pablo represent two extremes with regard to this question. Anselmo hates killing people in all circumstances, although he will do so if he must. Pablo, on the other hand, accepts killing as a part of his life and ultimately demonstrates that he is willing to kill his own men just to take their horses. Robert Jordan's position about killing falls somewhere between Anselmo's and Pablo's positions. Although Robert Jordan doesn't like to think about killing, he has killed many people in the line of duty. His personal struggle with this question ends on a note of compromise. Although war can't fully absolve him of guilt, and he has "no right to forget any of it," Robert Jordan knows both that he must kill people as part of his duties in the war, and that dwelling on his guilt during wartime is not productive.

The question of when it is justifiable to kill a person becomes complicated when we read that several characters, including Andrés, Agustín, Rafael, and even Robert Jordan, admit to experiencing a rush of excitement while killing. Hemingway does not take a clear moral stance regarding when it is acceptable to take another person's life. At times he even implies that killing can be exhilarating, which makes the morality of the war in *For Whom the Bell Tolls* even murkier.

Romantic Love as Salvation

Even though many of the characters in *For Whom the Bell Tolls* take a cynical view of human nature and feel fatigued by the war, the novel still holds out hope for romantic love. Even the worldly-wise Pilar, in her memories of Finito, reveals traces of a romantic, idealistic outlook on the world. Robert Jordan and Maria fall in love at first sight, and their love is grand and idealistic. Love endows Robert Jordan's life with new meaning and gives him new reasons to fight in the wake of the disillusionment he feels for the Republican cause. He believes in love despite the fact that other people—notably Karkov, who subscribes to the "purely materialistic" philosophy fashionable with the Hotel Gaylord set—reject its existence. This new acceptance of ideal, romantic love is one of the most important ways in which Robert Jordan rejects abstract theories in favor of intuition and action over the course of the novel.

Motifs

Motifs are recurring structures, contrasts, or literary devices that can help to develop and inform the text's major themes.

Rabbits and Hares

Animal imagery pervades *For Whom the Bell Tolls*, but rabbits and hares appear most frequently. Robert Jordan's nickname for Maria is "Rabbit." When Robert Jordan first meets Rafael, the gypsy is making traps for rabbits. Later, Rafael, distracted by trapping a pair of hares that he has caught mating in the snow, leaves his post. The guerrilla fighters have a somber meal of rabbit stew after the Fascists slaughter El Sordo's men. And shortly before his death, El Sordo invokes the image of a skinned rabbit when thinking about how vulnerable before enemy planes he feels on his hilltop.

The association of the *guerrilleros* with rabbits underscores their fragile position relative to the Fascists. Throughout the novel, we get the impression that the Fascists are the hunters and the *guerrilleros* the hunted: much like rabbits, Robert Jordan and his band are prey rather than predators. Like rabbits, the *guerrilleros* live in close contact with the natural world: they are a small, vulnerable group, in sharp contrast to the well-equipped Fascists with their incessant plane patrols and threatening, industrial war machinery.

The Forest Floor

For Whom the Bell Tolls opens with Robert Jordan lying "flat on the brown pine-needled floor of the forest." We see him amid the evergreens on the forest floor at several points throughout the novel, implying how he literally embraces the Spanish land. On the second night, after it snows, Robert Jordan makes a bed of spruce branches for himself and Maria to share. His embrace of Maria and his closeness to the ground becomes a physical act of love both for the woman and the country. Toward the end of the novel, Robert Jordan assumes his post as he awaits the start of the attack on the bridge. On he is again "on his belly behind the pine trunk" and feels the "give of the brown, dropped pine-needles under his elbows." His literal closeness to the earth highlights the natural, pre-civilized lifestyle that the guerrilla fighters lead in the wilderness. Robert Jordan takes this position one final time, at the very end of the novel, when he again lies behind a tree and feels "his heart beating against the pine needle floor the forest." Comparing his position at the end of the novel to his almost identical position at the beginning reminds us of the ways in which Robert Jordan has changed over the course of the novel. There is a new element at the end—his beating heart, which he has reawakened through his relationships with Maria and with the guerrilla fighters.

Signs and Omens

Omens abound in *For Whom the Bell Tolls*, and the belief in them indicate closeness to a pre-civilized, natural way of life. For example, the worry Pilar feels after reading Robert Jordan's palm is borne out when Robert Jordan is wounded at the end of the novel. Even characters who claim not to believe in signs often rely on them subconsciously. Although Robert Jordan professes not to believe Pilar's superstitions, he plays games with himself and repeatedly interprets natural phenomena as signs. His framing of other people's behaviors as good signs or bad signs further undermines his claim not to believe in omens. At the end of the novel, however, as Robert Jordan faces death and comes to terms with his life, he grudgingly admits that gypsies do indeed "see something . . . feel something." Ultimately, Hemingway implies that the wisdom associated with the natural, Spanish way of life trumps the other characters' cynical rationality and skepticism.

Suicide

Throughout *For Whom the Bell Tolls*, Hemingway characterizes suicide as an act of cowardice by associating it with characters who are vulnerable or lack strength of spirit. A number of characters contemplate suicide: Karkov always carries pills to use to kill himself if he is ever captured, and Maria carries around a razor blade for the same purpose. Robert Jordan's father committed suicide—an act that Robert Jordan says he understands but nonetheless condemns. The traits of these characters who contemplate suicide connect the act of suicide to weakness. Robert Jordan's father is characterized as weak, Maria is young and female, and Karkov is a man of ideas, not action. At the end of the novel, Robert Jordan contemplates suicide but rejects the idea, preferring to struggle to stay awake despite the pain. Robert Jordan's reliance on inner strength in his rejection of suicide contrasts the other characters' weakness, which demonstrates that the will to continue living requires psychological strength.

Symbols

Symbols are objects, characters, figures, or colors used to represent abstract ideas or concepts.

Planes, Tanks, and Mortars

The rumble of Fascist war machinery often jars the serenity of the Spanish mountains in *For Whom the Bell Tolls*, usually in the form of Italian and German observation and bomber planes that fly overhead. The military threat from the Fascists is both physical and moral: the planes menace not only with their bombs but also with their intimidating rumble. The planes move like "mechanized doom," conveying a sense of automation and industry that contrasts sharply with the earthy, close-to-nature lifestyle of Robert Jordan's relatively helpless band of guerrillas. The fact that the planes move like "mechanized doom" highlights the Fascists' superior technology. At the time of the Spanish Civil War, industrialization threatened the natural lifestyle of the peasants who lived off the land not only in Spain but also in many other countries. Hemingway saw Spain as one of the last places where small community life was still possible, and he saw the Spanish Civil War as destroying this possibility.

Absinthe

Robert Jordan's flask of absinthe (a green liqueur flavored with anise, a substance similar to licorice) embodies his deep appreciation for sensory pleasures—food, drink, smells, touch, sex, and so on. For Robert Jordan, absinthe "[takes] the place of the evening papers, of all the old evenings in cafés, of all the chestnut trees that would be in bloom now in this month . . . of all the things he had enjoyed and forgotten." Although Robert Jordan uses absinthe to buy trust and build relationships with the guerrilla fighters, he cannot help begrudging every drop. In the novel's wartime setting, absinthe represents the attitude that one should take advantage of carnal or sensory pleasures while one has the chance.

Summary & Analysis

Epigraph and Chapters One–Two

Summary: Epigraph
For Whom the Bell Tolls opens with an epigraph, a short quotation that introduces the novel, sets the mood, and presents a theme. This epigraph is from a short essay by the seventeenth-century British poet John Donne. Donne writes that no person stands alone—"No man is an island, entire of itself"—because everyone belongs to a community. As a result, the death of any human diminishes Donne himself because he is a part of mankind. Donne admonishes us not to ask who has died when we hear a funeral bell toll, for it tolls for everyone in the human race.

Summary: Chapter One
On a Saturday afternoon in May 1937, a young man and an old peasant named Anselmo survey the Spanish countryside from the side of a hill. The young man is Robert Jordan, an American university instructor fighting on the Republican side against the Fascists during the Spanish Civil War. Anselmo is guiding Robert Jordan behind enemy lines to join a small band of guerrilla fighters near the bridge that Robert Jordan has been instructed to blow up.

Anselmo leaves Robert Jordan near a stream outside the camp and goes ahead to warn the other guerrilla fighters that a stranger is approaching. As he waits for Anselmo to return, Robert Jordan thinks back on the night before, when he received his bridge-blowing assignment from the Russian General Golz. Golz explained that the bridge operation is part of a larger Republican offensive to take the city of Segovia. The bridge must be blown up on Tuesday morning, after aerial bombardment begins. Both Golz and Robert Jordan understood that the assignment was difficult.

Anselmo returns with Pablo, the leader of the guerrilla camp. Pablo is openly hostile to Robert Jordan, who shows the illiterate Pablo identification papers that Pablo cannot read. Pablo challenges Robert Jordan's plan to blow up the bridge and refuses to help carry the packs full of dynamite until Anselmo scolds him.

At the top of the mountain, the three men pass Pablo's makeshift corral of five horses that his guerrilla band has found or stolen.

Pablo tests Robert Jordan's knowledge of horses by asking him to identify which of the five horses is lame. Anselmo recalls the last major guerrilla operation, the bombing of an enemy train, which Pablo and a Russian operative named Kashkin carried out. Robert Jordan reveals that Kashkin is now dead. Pablo says that he doesn't want to follow Robert Jordan's orders.

Robert Jordan thinks to himself that Pablo's sadness is a sign that Pablo is losing his loyalty to the Republican cause. Robert Jordan predicts that Pablo will betray the Republican cause. Robert Jordan believes that he will know when Pablo has made a decision to betray the guerrillas because Pablo will suddenly start to be nice. Robert Jordan dismisses his thoughts and looks forward to dinner.

Summary: Chapter Two

In front of the cave that functions as the headquarters of Pablo's camp, Robert Jordan meets Rafael, an old gypsy who traps rabbits. They drink wine, smoke Robert Jordan's Russian cigarettes, and await their food. Robert Jordan tells the others that Kashkin committed suicide when he was captured, but he conceals the details. Robert Jordan thinks to himself that Kashkin did more harm than good because he let the fighters know that he was nervous.

A young, short-haired woman named Maria brings food out of the cave. Self-conscious about her haircut, she explains that she once had long hair, but that Fascists cut it short when they captured her recently. She was on the Fascist train that Pablo and Kashkin blew up, and afterward she rejoined the guerrilla fighters. Robert Jordan feels drawn to Maria and finds out that she is not married.

After Maria leaves, Rafael tells Robert Jordan about their seven-man, two-woman camp and their machine gun. Rafael says that Pilar, Pablo's "woman," insisted that they take in Maria. Rafael recounts how exhilarating the train operation was and describes the engine hurtling through the air like a "great wounded animal." Rafael says that he manned the machine gun.

The half-gypsy Pilar, stocky and brusque, emerges from the cave. She makes Robert Jordan promise to take Maria with him when he leaves. Pilar then reads Robert Jordan's palm and seems troubled by what she sees. Despite his claims not to be superstitious, he wants to know what Pilar sees. Pilar says that a nearby guerrilla band, led by a man named El Sordo, will be able to help with the bridge. Anselmo and Robert Jordan prepare to leave to inspect the bridge.

Analysis: Epigraph and Chapters One–Two

Together, the title and the epigraph, from which the title comes, announce two of the main themes of *For Whom the Bell Tolls*: the role of an individual within a community and the value of human life, especially in a time of war. The funeral bell of the title and epigraph introduce the idea of human mortality, a reminder that all human beings are destined to die. Because everyone belongs to humanity, the metaphorical bell that announces one individual's death also announces the death of something within everyone. Humankind is inextricably united in this way, so that the loss of any one part affects the whole. The fear of death looms large in the novel, for the characters are involved in a wartime guerrilla operation that is up against considerable odds. The reminder of death inherent in the title and the epigraph sets the tone for the characters' anxieties about death and the novel's celebration of life.

The conflict between Pablo and Robert Jordan, which arises virtually from the moment they first meet, develops into one of the central thematic conflicts of the novel. Pablo, a man of reckless individuality, proudly announces that his primary responsibility is to himself. He will not participate in bridge-blowing, regardless of how important the operation may be for the Republic. Robert Jordan, in contrast, has voluntarily left a cushy life in America to fight in a foreign war. Even though he also has reservations about the bridge operation, he nevertheless is committed to carrying it out. He feels it is his duty, he knows his general is counting on him, and he retains some hope despite all odds that the larger Republican offensive will be a success. Just as Pablo and Robert Jordan disagree over whether or not to blow up the bridge, the larger ideas that the two men represent—individualism versus community involvement—come into conflict throughout the novel.

Kashkin, Robert Jordan's predecessor in the forest, functions as a foil (a character whose actions or attitudes contrast with those of another, highlighting the differences between them) to Robert Jordan. Whereas Robert Jordan is steady and in control, Kashkin was nervous, especially about his own death—in the *guerrilleros*' terminology, Kashkin had "gone bad." The differences between the two men make Robert Jordan's cool-headedness more pronounced. Kashkin functions as a cautionary figure for Robert Jordan, making him aware that, as a leader, his attitude affects those he leads. Kashkin's nervousness rubbed off on his guerrillas, so he did more harm than good. Also,

Kashkin's capture and death remind us of the danger of Robert Jordan's work and suggest that a similar fate might befall him.

The opening of the novel strips Hemingway's famously uncluttered, simple writing style even more bare than usual. Initially, we know neither the names of the two characters nor what they are doing in the forest. The narrator makes no comment on the action and restricts observations to the physical world—what an observer might see, hear, or smell. The names Anselmo and Roberto (as Robert Jordan initially calls himself) are revealed to us on a need-to-know basis, at the same time as they are revealed to the characters. The impression that we are eavesdropping, watching a scene unfolding here and now, creates dramatic tension because we want to figure out what is going on. Typical of Hemingway's style, the characters seem to leave very much unsaid. It is not until Anselmo leaves and Robert Jordan is alone that we are allowed to enter Robert Jordan's head to know his thoughts.

Throughout the novel, Hemingway uses older English vocabulary and a number of grammatical structures that are more typical of Spanish than English. These word choices and structures recreate the spirit of the Spanish language, emphasizing its deep connection with the past and giving the novel a distant and heroic flavor. Odd-sounding phrases like "the woman of Pablo" and "I informed myself from the gypsy" give the impression that the novel was written in Spanish and has been translated word for word, retaining Spanish grammar. Hemingway's Spanish was not particularly strong—the Spanish in *For Whom the Bell Tolls* is notoriously riddled with errors—so he uses the language in order to evoke the spirit of his setting rather than to add authenticity to the novel. The older English forms that Hemingway uses—words like "thou," "art," "dost"—lend a pre-modern, natural aura to the characters in Robert Jordan's band of *guerrilleros* and to the novel as a whole.

Chapters Three–Seven

Summary: Chapter Three

Robert Jordan and Anselmo scout out the bridge. Robert Jordan watches a sentry on the bridge through binoculars and notes that he has a "peasant face." Fascist planes fly overhead, but Robert Jordan lets Anselmo think that they are Republican planes. The two men discuss war and religion. Anselmo likes to hunt but hates killing people, whereas Robert Jordan hates killing animals but is willing to kill people when required. They recall that gypsies and Native Americans both view bears as man's brothers. Anselmo says that he misses believing in God. Robert Jordan silently resents his mission and thinks about Maria.

On the way back, Robert Jordan and Anselmo meet Agustín, another of Pablo's band, who stands guard but has forgotten his half of the password. Agustín cautions Robert Jordan to watch his explosives. When they are alone again, Anselmo says that Agustín is trustworthy, but Pablo is "bad."

SUMMARY: CHAPTER FOUR

Back at camp, Robert Jordan brings his backpacks into the cave, where the atmosphere is tense. Pablo says that there is little wine left, so Robert Jordan drinks from his own flask of absinthe. Robert Jordan meets three more band members, Primitivo and the brothers Andrés and Eladio.

Pablo announces that he refuses to blow up the bridge. Robert Jordan replies that he and Anselmo will do it alone. Pilar announces that she supports the bridge operation because she supports the Republic. The men back Pilar, and she says that she is the real leader of the group. Pablo gives in sullenly. Robert Jordan shows the others his plans for the bridge. Looking at Pablo, Pilar is momentarily filled with sorrow and foreboding.

SUMMARY: CHAPTER FIVE

After dinner, Robert Jordan steps outside the cave into the night air. Inside, Rafael sings a song making fun of Catalans (members of a Spanish ethnic subgroup) but Pablo interrupts him. Rafael joins Robert Jordan outside and says that Robert Jordan should have killed Pablo during the confrontation earlier. Robert Jordan says that he considered it but did not want to risk alienating the other band members.

Meanwhile, Pablo fondly confides in one of his horses. The narrator notes that the horse does not understand what Pablo says.

SUMMARY: CHAPTER SIX

Back inside the cave, Pilar says that Robert Jordan is too serious. He replies that he is anti-Fascist rather than Communist. Then, he seems uncomfortable discussing his father's suicide. Maria admits that she is attracted to Robert Jordan, and he strokes her head. In private, he asks Pilar whether he should have killed Pablo. She assures him Pablo is no longer dangerous.

Summary: Chapter Seven

Robert Jordan sleeps in a robe outside the cave. Around one o'clock in the morning, Maria wakes him and slips in with him under the robe. He tries to kiss her, but she is nervous. She says she should not sleep with him if he does not love her. He says that he loves her, and she says that she loves him. Maria tells Robert Jordan that she was raped several times, but that Pilar told her that having sex with someone she loved would heal her memory of the rape. He shows her how to kiss, and they make love.

Analysis: Chapters Three–Seven

For Whom the Bell Tolls is preoccupied with signs and omens, and this section reveals several instances of foreshadowing that both heighten the drama and set the tone. Agustín's warning to Robert Jordan to pay close attention to his packs explicitly increases the suspense and foreshadows Pablo's later betrayal. In contrast, Pilar's sense of sadness upon looking at Pablo after the men have sworn their allegiance to her establishes mood in a less specific manner. Both types of foreshadowing establish an atmosphere of foreboding for the future, and both make future events appear predictable and inevitable. In particular, Pilar's sense of sadness is rooted in the idea that human nature does not change and the idea that history repeats itself. This sense of predictability and repetitiveness contributes to the grim, ominous mood that pervades the novel.

The poignant scene between Pablo and his horse sheds more light on the opposition between Robert Jordan's sense of community and Pablo's isolation. Misunderstood and lonely, Pablo complains to and seeks comfort from his horse, a creature that belongs to the natural world and remains untainted by the petty struggles of humans. As we might expect, and as the narrator subsequently reveals, the horse does not understand Pablo. The narrator drives home Pablo's isolation with the revelation that the horse actually finds Pablo bothersome and wishes he would go away. Whereas Pablo fails in his attempt to communicate with his horse using words, Robert Jordan is successful in his nearly wordless communication with Maria. Robert Jordan eases the pain of Maria's past sexual trauma, whereas the horse does nothing to ease Pablo's emotional burden.

Hemingway cleanly divides his moral world into characters who are "good," such as Robert Jordan, Anselmo, Pilar, and Agustín; and those who are "bad," such as Pablo. Because Hemingway reiterates these classifications many times through many different characters, we can rely on it to infer that "good" qualities include competence, steady nerves, honesty with oneself, and loyalty. On the other hand, "bad" qualities include fear, greed, pessimism, and self-delusion. Two characters—Rafael and Maria—notably escape this moral classification. Both Rafael, a full-blooded gypsy, and Maria, a young woman, belong to groups that Spanish society marginalized at the time. Rafael is repeatedly characterized as well-meaning but "worthless," which puts his character in an ambiguous middle ground. Similarly, Maria comes across as a somewhat weak and flimsy character, in part because she is a naïve young woman. In this way, Hemingway's seemingly rigid moral classifications exclude people who exist only on the margins of the world he portrays.

Robert Jordan, in particular, conforms to a character type that recurs throughout Hemingway's novels—a character commonly referred to as the "code hero" because he follows the Hemingway moral code. The code hero's most prominent characteristic is his ability to exhibit what Hemingway called "grace under pressure." The code hero lives life for the present and takes his pleasure in the physical world of food, sex, and nature. He is a man of action rather than thought, and his greatest triumph is conquering his fear of death and nothingness (which some critics term nada after the Spanish word for "nothing"). Robert Jordan's appreciation for nature and physical experiences—the smell of the pine trees, the taste of absinthe that evokes Paris, his coupling with Maria—indicates that he fits the code hero type, at least to some degree. For the time being, however, we see that Robert Jordan experiences many unresolved tensions that he tries to work through in his head. At this point, it is unclear whether he is a man of thought or action.

Chapters Eight–Thirteen

Summary: Chapter Eight

By dawn, Maria is gone. Robert Jordan goes back to sleep until the sound of enemy airplanes wakes him. A total of forty-five planes fly overhead, in groups of threes and nines. Robert Jordan wonders whether the Fascists know about the planned guerrilla offensive, so he sends Anselmo to watch the road.

At breakfast, Fernando, the ninth member of the band, reports that the night before, he heard rumors about a possible Republican offensive in La Granja, the nearest town. Pilar talks about a time when she visited the city of Valencia when her lover, Finito, had a bullfighting gig there. After breakfast, the sound of enemy planes returns.

Summary: Chapter Nine

Three enemy planes fly very low overhead. Robert Jordan promises Pilar that he will be careful with Maria. Pilar tells him that during the night, after she and Pablo made love, she heard Pablo crying because his men had renounced his leadership. In private, Agustín tells Pilar that he does not trust Pablo, but even so, he wants Pablo to plan their retreat after they blow up the bridge.

Summary: Chapter Ten

Pilar, Maria, and Robert Jordan leave to visit El Sordo and talk to him about the bridge operation. They stop to rest along the way. Pilar complains that she is ugly, even though she admits that she has had many lovers in her life.

Pilar then tells a long story about the start of the war in Pablo's hometown. After shooting four Fascist guards point blank, Pablo orchestrated a brutal scenario to kill the town Fascists. Pilar compares the situation to bull-baiting. Pablo and his cohorts forced each Fascist to walk past a line of Republican peasants, who beat him with flails before throwing him off a cliff. The last remaining Fascists and the priest overseeing them prayed inside a holding cell until Pablo unlocked the door and a mob rushed in and tore them apart. Afterward, Pablo expressed disappointment with the priest's lack of dignity. That night, Pablo and Pilar abstained from having sex. Pilar says that that day, along with the day three days later, when the Fascists retook the town, were the worst of her life. Pilar's story reminds Robert Jordan of a time when he saw the lynching of a black man in Ohio when he was seven years old.

Summary: Chapter Eleven

A young man named Joaquín, who guards El Sordo's camp, greets Robert Jordan, Pilar, and Maria. Joaquín and Maria joke about the time when Joaquín carried her after the *guerrilleros* blew up the Fascist train she was riding as a captive. Joaquín tells the others that Fascists killed his family. Robert Jordan thinks about the effect that his military missions have had on Republican peasants in small towns. Maria tells Joaquín that they all are his family now, and Pilar makes a point to include Robert Jordan.

Robert Jordan and Pilar speak to El Sordo, a nearly deaf man of few words, and enlist his aid in blowing up the bridge. Robert Jordan reveals that he killed the wounded Kashkin at Kashkin's request. He and El Sordo discuss supplies and tactics, especially the unfortunate fact that they must carry out the bridge operation in daylight because the attack is part of a larger offensive. The daylight timing will make it much more difficult to retreat. They speak about retreating to the Gredos mountain range, though Pilar wants to flee to Republican-controlled territory.

SUMMARY: CHAPTER TWELVE

On the way back to Pablo's camp, Pilar is irritable and looks pale. She tells Maria that she is jealous of Maria's youth and beauty and that she begrudges having to leave Maria to Robert Jordan. As promised, Pilar leaves them. Robert Jordan wants to follow Pilar, but Maria convinces him to let her go.

SUMMARY: CHAPTER THIRTEEN

> *For him it was a dark passage which led to nowhere, then to nowhere, then again to nowhere, once again to nowhere, always and forever to nowhere ...*
> *(See* QUOTATIONS, *p. 59)*

Robert Jordan and Maria make love in the forest. Afterward, as they walk to catch up with Pilar, Maria says that she dies each time they make love. Both acknowledge having felt the earth move. Maria continues talking, but Robert Jordan thinks about his work. He feels completely indifferent to political matters now. He believes that he fights with the Communists not because he believes in their doctrine but because it is the best side to be on in this particular war. The Republicans will have to do a lot to organize their government. He wonders about the possibility that the Republican leaders are in some ways the "enemies" of their own people.

Robert Jordan wonders if he could possibly take Maria back with him to Montana to be his wife—or even whether he himself, as a Communist, might be unwelcome there. He wants to write a book about what he has seen in the war. He thinks that perhaps these days in the mountains might be his whole, full life. When he pays attention to Maria again, she shows him the razor blade she carries around in case she should be captured. She tells him that she will take care of him.

Robert Jordan and Maria catch up with Pilar, who bullies Maria into telling her that earth moved during their lovemaking. Pilar says that such a thing can happen only three times in a lifetime. Robert

Jordan tells Pilar to focus less on mysteries and more on work. As they travel, Pilar observes that it is going to snow, despite the fact that it is late in May.

Analysis: Chapters Eight–Thirteen

The planes flying overhead represent a menace to the *guerrilleros*, to the Republican cause, and to the natural world and the simple way of life in general. Impressive in size and aggressive in behavior, the planes search the mountains and carry bombs that present a very real threat to the lives of the guerrilla fighters. The planes' German and Italian make reminds us that the Fascist side has powerful European allies. The Republicans, on the other hand, have only volunteer foreign units under the umbrella of the International Brigades. The sheer number of planes attests to the Fascist military might and foreshadows the eventual Republican defeat. Hemingway makes the threat more vivid by comparing the planes to "sharks" and calling them "mechanized doom." As symbols of not only military prowess but also modern industrial power, the planes also pose a threat to the serenity of the natural world and the simple way of life that Hemingway celebrates in the novel.

Pilar's brutal story about the massacre at Pablo's village shows that neither side is innocent in the war. Both sides have committed unspeakable atrocities. As Pilar describes, Pablo's village was ravaged twice—the first time by Pablo and his Republican cohorts, the second time, three days later, by the Fascists who return to retake the village and exact revenge. The two sides act in the same reprehensible way, which makes it difficult for us to see either side as morally superior. This moral confusion is one of the key ways in which the twentieth-century war novel differs from its predecessors. War novels of the nineteenth century and earlier tended to portray war in a romanticized light, as an institution that rewarded honor and offered the opportunity for great glory. But after the senseless and widespread destruction of World War I, novels such as Erich Maria Remarque's *All Quiet on the Western Front* deflated the glorious myth of war and exposed the realistic horrors of the battlefield. *For Whom the Bell Tolls* falls solidly in this second category, as a realistic portrayal shows that neither side was particularly honorable.

Pilar's story also demonstrates the strong connection between sex and death that runs throughout *For Whom the Bell Tolls*. After the massacre of the Fascists in his hometown, Pablo decides to refrain from sex with Pilar. Hemingway uses this connection to show that killing is similar to a sexual experience, both physically and psychologically. Because Pablo has just taken part in a massacre, he no longer needs to have sex with Pilar; his lack of sexual desire implies he satisfied his sexual desire by killing. Indeed, later in the novel, when Andrés recalls baiting a bull, Hemingway uses sexual language to describe the event, writing, "he . . . drove his knife again and again and again into the swelling . . . bulge of the neck that was now spouting hot on his fist." Furthermore, just as Hemingway portrays killing as another form of sexual experience, he likewise portrays sex as a form of death. Maria's comment that she "dies" each time she and Robert Jordan make love equates her sexual experience with the experience of Pablo's and Andrés's victims. The similarity of the descriptions of the two experiences argues that they are interchangeable in their degree of emotional intensity.

Robert Jordan's comments to Maria show that, unlike her, he is unable to give his heart fully. Whereas Maria says that she "dies" each time they make love, Robert Jordan remarks that he only "almost" dies. "Death" within the context of a sexual experience entails a complete loss of senses and complete trust in one's partner. Robert Jordan's inability to "die" points to his inability to let go completely with Maria. Especially in a time of war, he must always be on guard. Before the first time that they make love, Robert Jordan remarks that the stress of his mission makes it difficult for him to fully immerse himself in Maria: "I cannot have a woman doing what I do." He believes that he cannot be true to his mission and be concerned about her at the same time. His inability to achieve complete communion with Maria is one of the tensions in his life. It is Maria's patience at hearing these partial rejections that ultimately allows Robert Jordan to resolve this tension.

Robert Jordan and Maria's sensation that earth moves during their lovemaking frames their love affair as part of a larger natural cycle. The fact that the lovers feel the earth move—one popular interpretation is that Robert Jordan and Maria experience a simultaneous orgasm—creates the impression that nature itself blesses their love. Pilar's insistence that such an earth-moving experience occurs no more than three times in a lifetime connects the lovers' experience to an ancient, close-to-the-earth culture. However, decay is an inevitable part of the natural cycle in which Robert Jordan and Maria participate, which means that death will strike eventually. Just as Pilar has lost youth and beauty, which makes her jealous of the young Maria, so must Robert Jordan lose his vitality as time passes.

One critic suggests that Robert Jordan and Maria feel the earth move because in their coupling they manage, for a brief instant, literally to stop the course of time in the narrative. Because the lovers begin their relationship during wartime and know that Robert Jordan will have to face grave danger within days, time is the most valuable commodity for them—and stopping time is the ultimate bliss. Because they lack time, their courtship is accelerated, and they declare their love for each other within hours of meeting. Momentarily frozen in time and space, immersed in the moment when they make love, they are able to feel the very movement of the Earth rotating on its axis and revolving around the sun. This interpretation casts the Earth itself, rather than folk wisdom, as Robert Jordan and Maria's guardian.

Chapters Fourteen–Seventeen

Summary: Chapter Fourteen
By the time Pilar, Maria, and Robert Jordan return to camp, it has already begun to snow. Pablo predicts that a great deal of snow will fall. Inwardly, Robert Jordan briefly feels enraged and disgusted by his mission and the whole war, but he quickly calms down. Pablo tells Robert Jordan that he used to take care of horses for Finito, Pilar's former companion, who was a bullfighter. Pilar tells a story about a time when one bull hit Finito particularly hard during a fight. Finito made a scene at a dinner in his honor that was held after the bullfight. That winter, Finito died.

After Pilar finishes her story, Rafael returns from his watch and makes a report. Fernando volunteers to take Robert Jordan to pick up Anselmo, who is watching the road.

Summary: Chapter Fifteen
Despite the snowstorm, Anselmo still mans his post. He watches Fascist soldiers who are headquartered inside a sawmill across the road. He realizes that the soldiers are poor peasants just like him. He remembers the first time he killed a man, which was during a raid that Pablo organized.

Meanwhile, inside the sawmill, a corporal and three Fascist soldiers talk about the snow and the superiority of the Fascists' air power. Outside, Anselmo is cold and lonely and misses praying. Finally, Robert Jordan and Fernando arrive and escort Anselmo back to the camp. Robert Jordan is happy that Anselmo has stayed at his post through the snowstorm.

Summary: Chapter Sixteen
Back in the cave, Pilar tells Robert Jordan that El Sordo stopped by and then left to find more horses. Maria attentively waits on Robert Jordan, who is pleased and touched that El Sordo has brought him whiskey. Pablo, drinking in the corner, alternately insults Robert Jordan and voices mournful thoughts. In particular, Pablo expresses regret for the massacre of the Fascists in his hometown.

To defuse the tension, Primitivo and the other men ask Robert Jordan questions about his job teaching Spanish and about American social policy. Robert Jordan tries to provoke Pablo into a fight, thinking it would be an opportune moment to kill Pablo and not have the other men turn against him. Pablo refuses to take the bait, however. Agustín hits Pablo several times in the face and calls him a horse-lover, but Pablo remains calm. Finally, Pablo goes out to check on his horses.

Summary: Chapter Seventeen
While Pablo is outside, the group in the cave discusses what to do with him. Rafael suggests selling Pablo to the Fascists, but the rest agree that he should be killed. Robert Jordan volunteers to do it that night. At that moment, Pablo returns, grinning, and asks if they were speaking about him. He resumes drinking wine. He announces offhandedly that he will help with the bridge operation. Pilar indicates to Robert Jordan that she is sure that Pablo overheard them discussing the plan to kill him.

Analysis: Chapters Fourteen–Seventeen
Hemingway uses the character of Finito both as a foil for Pablo and to illustrate his deep appreciation for Spanish culture and the art of bullfighting. Finito's bravery in the ring despite his fear of the bulls reinforces Hemingway's theory that, because bullfighters face death in their daily lives, they get used to their fear of death and conquer it. Finito is thus a prime example of the Hemingway bullfighter—one who, by nature, has fears like anyone else but still knows how to act bravely. Indeed, Finito's natural fear only makes him more courageous in having become a bullfighter. Hemingway's theory extends to all Spaniards: because Spaniards often see a man facing death in a bullfight, they learn to face their fear of death. No longer crippled by this fear, they are able to live fuller lives. In this regard, Finito is a

foil for Pablo, who fears death. By comparing Pablo to the bulls that Finito used to kill, Pilar explicitly contrasts Finito's bravery, learned with difficulty in the bullring, with Pablo's temporary fierceness, which is fueled more by wine than any real bravery.

The similarity between the Fascist guards at the sawmill and the Republican guerrilla fighters shows the arbitrariness of the line that divides the two sides. The soldiers at the sawmill discuss the same topics the guerrilla fighters discuss—the weather, evil omens, the enemy's planes. Like the guerrilla fighters, the Fascist soldiers rely on nature to keep track of time. The ordinary quality of these conversation topics underscores the Fascist soldiers' humanity. As Anselmo notices, the Fascists are peasants just like him. He realizes that the soldiers probably landed on the Fascist side only by chance, because they lived in territories the Fascists controlled. Chance has played a role in the selection of guerrilla fighters too: Andrés later reflects that he probably would have become a Fascist soldier if his father hadn't been a Republican—and that it would have been just as well either way. Because the composition of the armies arises from an accident of fate, neither side can claim to have the moral upper hand. This lack of moral clarity makes the question of killing people—even within the context of war—particularly problematic. The sawmill scene specifically illustrates the unfairness, arbitrariness, and moral confusion of the Spanish Civil War and of modern war in general.

Anselmo's longing for prayer highlights the fact that the Republican leadership has outlawed religion—a policy Robert Jordan sees as a betrayal of the Spanish people. In Robert Jordan's view, the Republic has taken religion away from its people but given them nothing to replace the void. Older Spaniards like Anselmo, who have been religious their whole lives, now have no comfort in their old age. Later in the novel, Anselmo and several younger characters, like Joaquín, find themselves turning to prayer during traumatic moments. This turn to prayer is evidence that the Republic has failed them, since, in praying, they break a useless Republican law. In the end, religious faith and prayer prevail over loyalty to the state—in moments of crisis, people perform actions that reflect their true colors rather than skin-deep political allegiances.

Chapters Eighteen–Twenty

Summary: Chapter Eighteen

You felt that you were taking part in a crusade.... It gave you a part in something that you could believe in wholly and completely.
(See Quotations, p. 60)

Robert Jordan feels that his confrontations with Pablo recur as though they were on a merry-go-round. He finishes drawing up plans for blowing up the bridge. He imagines going to Madrid after blowing up the bridge, staying at the Florida Hotel, and dining at Gaylord's, the gathering place for important Russian expatriates in Madrid. It was at Gaylord's that Robert Jordan began to learn insider information, such as the fact that many Spanish Republican leaders had been trained in Russia or came from more privileged backgrounds than they let on. Although these deceptions and the opulence at Gaylord's initially made Robert Jordan uncomfortable, he has come to understand that the deceptions are necessary and that the opulence is nice.

At Gaylord's, Robert Jordan met Karkov, an intelligent journalist for the Russian newspaper *Pravda* with great taste in women. The two men became friends. Robert Jordan remembers that Karkov was at one point responsible for three wounded Russians who were being held captive in the city. If Madrid were taken by the Fascists, Karkov was to poison the three men so that no evidence of Russian involvement would remain. Karkov said that it was not a difficult task to poison someone if you were used to always carrying poison you might have to use on yourself.

Thinking of Karkov, Robert Jordan remembers another scene. During an attack on Madrid, Robert Jordan dragged a dead man out of a car only to abandon him in the street as the dead man's partner wanted. He abandoned the body in order to go assist a third man who was dying of an arm wound nearby. Moments afterward, Robert Jordan was stopped by a well-known British economist named Mitchell, whom Robert Jordan recognized but had never met before. Mitchell offered a cigarette and asked for information about the war, but Robert Jordan swore at him, disgusted with his academic airs. Robert Jordan remembers discussing Mitchell with Karkov. Karkov suggested that Robert Jordan read up on philosophy. Karkov also said that he read Robert Jordan's one published academic book and said that he liked its writing style. Robert Jordan resolves to write another book about the things he knows now, the things he has come to learn in the war, which are "not so simple."

Summary: Chapter Nineteen
Maria interrupts Robert Jordan's musings. In front of everyone, Pilar says that Robert Jordan shot Kashkin. Pilar claims that Kashkin had a premonition that he would die, and that he smelled of death. Robert Jordan, who claims that he does not believe in superstitions, says it was more of a self-fulfilling prophecy for the nervous Kashkin.

Pilar describes the smell of death, which has four main components: the brass on a ship in danger of sinking, the taste of the kiss of an old woman who has drunk the blood of a slaughtered animal, dead flowers in the trash, and dirty water from a brothel. The snowstorm ends.

Summary: Chapter Twenty
Outside, Robert Jordan makes a bed out of a spruce tree. He lies in the bed, thinking about soul-calming smells, and waits for Maria. She comes barefoot through the snow wearing her nightgown, which she calls her "wedding shirt." Their pillow-talk revolves around the idea that they are one and share the same heart. They make love, and Maria says that this coupling was different from the afternoon's. In the middle of the night, Robert Jordan wakes up and embraces her, then moves away and thinks.

Analysis: Chapters Eighteen–Twenty
The merry-go-round image that Robert Jordan uses to describe his frustrations with Pablo is just one of many cyclical structures in *For Whom the Bell Tolls*. One critic has called this merry-go-round "the wheel of human conflict." The novel as a whole follows a circular path. As we see in the final chapter, the story ends in the forest where it began, with Robert Jordan lying on the pine needle-covered ground, watching and waiting. The novel marks a cycle in Robert Jordan's life—a fact Robert Jordan calls attention to in his musings that he's living the whole of his life in the three days portrayed in the novel. Indeed, a circle is a particularly apt shape to symbolize many of the novel's events. Robert Jordan's encounters with Maria, for instance, follow a cyclical pattern—they come together at night and part during the day. The circle also describes the structure of many natural phenomena observed in the novel, such as the movement of

the earth during the course of a day and the falling and melting of late-May snow. The merry-go-round image represents a literal version of these cycles that run throughout in the novel.

Robert Jordan's memories of Madrid, especially the incident with the British economist Mitchell, illustrate Robert Jordan's inner tension between abstract theories and concrete action. Robert Jordan was rude when Mitchell asked for information about the war because Mitchell, busy with his theories far from the difficult physical realities of the war, couldn't possibly have had any conception of what the true experience of the war was like. In contrast, Robert Jordan, just before the conversation with Mitchell, had abandoned one dead man in order to save another wounded man. The contrast between Robert Jordan's competent actions backed by difficult moral decisions—abandoning one man's body in order to help another—and the economist's detached, academic interest is jarring. This incident illustrates that, at heart, Robert Jordan is a man of action, even if he often gets stuck in thinking about theories. In his impatience with Mitchell and his rejection of Karkov's suggestion that he read up on philosophy, Robert Jordan shows that he favors action over theory. We see this trait grow in Robert Jordan as the story progresses, and it is a major part of the development of his character over the course of the novel.

The conversation about the smell of death gives the novel an air of belonging to an older, earthier, pre-Christian time, when people believed the natural cycles of life to have mystical powers. In Pilar's graphic description, the ingredients for the smell of death all relate to primordial human experiences: nausea, fear of death, killing, the decay of beauty, and sex. Pilar says that the final ingredient contains "the smell that is both the death and birth of man"—experiences shared by all humans. Just like her earlier belief in palm-reading and the movement of the earth, Pilar's belief in a particular smell associated with death ties her to that older, pagan world. Also, many cultural traditions consider women to be more engaged with nature and its mysterious processes, at least in part because of their ability to give birth. Hemingway establishes these connections with nature in order to set up a framework for interpreting the development of Robert Jordan's character. In the growth of his relationship with Maria and in his acceptance of Pilar's gypsy superstitions, Robert Jordan turns away from the constraints imposed by modern society and moves toward nature and natural values.

Chapters Twenty-one–Twenty-six

Summary: Chapter Twenty-one

It is Monday morning. Robert Jordan hears the sound of hoof beats and sees a Fascist soldier on horseback riding toward him. He tells Maria to hide under the robe and then shoots the soldier. Everyone in the camp wakes. Robert Jordan asks who was supposed to be on guard. Pilar says it was Rafael, but Rafael is missing. Robert Jordan yells to the others to set up the machine gun and sends Pablo off with the Fascist soldier's horse so that the tracks will lead away from the camp. Distracted and busy, Robert Jordan refuses to tell Maria that he loves her.

Summary: Chapter Twenty-two

In the forest, Agustín, Primitivo, and Robert Jordan set up the machine gun and camouflage it with pine branches. Robert Jordan tells the others where to set it up and how to use it. He worries that because the snowstorm has stopped, the tracks that El Sordo made the night before will still be visible.

Rafael finally returns to his post. He was off trapping a pair of hares who were mating in the snow. Robert Jordan is disgusted but not angry. Rafael goes down to give the hares to the camp, and Primitivo mounts the hill a little higher to keep watch. Robert Jordan keeps an eye on two crows in nearby trees and decides that if the crows stay quiet, no one will come. One crow flies away. Robert Jordan discusses the next day's attack plan with Agustín. An observation plane rumbles overhead, and the second crow flies away.

Summary: Chapter Twenty-three

> *We do it coldly but they do not, nor ever have. It is their extra sacrament....*   (See Quotations, p. 61)

As Anselmo returns with more tree camouflage, Robert Jordan spots a group of four Fascist cavalrymen following the tracks of the Fascist horse Pablo led away. Robert Jordan insists that the other men—Agustín, Anselmo, and, on the hill above, Primitivo—stay quiet and not fire. The cavalry passes without noticing them. Another, larger group of horsemen also passes without seeing anything.

Anselmo volunteers to sneak to the nearby village of La Granja after the snow melts to find out any information he can. Robert Jordan is nervous and feels that he and the others are talking too much.

Agustín talks about the urge to kill that he felt as the cavalry rode by. Robert Jordan acknowledges to himself that he too has felt the excitement of killing. Anselmo says he would rather put prisoners to work than kill them. Anselmo then goes down to the camp to intercept Rafael and bring back breakfast.

Summary: Chapter Twenty-four
Over breakfast, Robert Jordan and Agustín talk about Maria. Agustín confides that he too is in love with her and implores Robert Jordan to take her love seriously. They discuss the dependability of their comrades. Agustín says that El Sordo's men are very good. Suddenly, Robert Jordan hushes Agustín. He hears noises in the distance and realizes that there is fighting at El Sordo's. He tells Agustín that they must not go to help but rather stay where they are.

Summary: Chapter Twenty-five
Primitivo, maddened by the sound of fighting on El Sordo's hill, is desperate to ride to help his comrades fight. Robert Jordan insists that doing so would be a useless sacrifice. He tells Primitivo that in war one must learn to handle such situations. Pilar arrives and supports Robert Jordan's decision. She mocks Primitivo for making a big deal out of the experience with the cavalrymen earlier in the morning. However, Pilar herself becomes quite shaken up when the three of them must hide from yet another low-flying observation plane. She apologizes to Primitivo for taking his fear lightly. Pilar leaves, promising to send Maria with the papers belonging to the Fascist horseman who Robert Jordan shot that morning.

Summary: Chapter Twenty-six
By noon, the last of the snow has melted. Robert Jordan reads letters from the dead cavalryman's sister and fiancée. He asks Primitivo if he wants to read them as well, but Primitivo replies that he is illiterate.

Robert Jordan argues with himself about how many people he has killed and whether killing them was justified—especially since most of them, like the cavalryman, were not true Fascists but poor peasants. Robert Jordan thinks that he is not a real Marxist because he believes in life, liberty, and the pursuit of happiness. He tells himself to feel lucky for having found Maria and wonders about the situation on El Sordo's hill. At three o'clock in the afternoon, more planes fly overhead.

Analysis: Chapters Twenty-one–Twenty-six

Robert Jordan's small but repeated rejections of Maria, in spite of his deep feelings for her, underscore the novel's tension between love and work, heart and head. Even though she asks him directly, Robert Jordan refuses to tell Maria that he loves her while he is focused on his work. Similarly, as he lies awake in bed the previous night, he cannot embrace Maria and think at the same time, so he moves away. Robert Jordan's refusal to admit his love in these situations reveals a split in his psyche. Robert Jordan is not yet whole as a person; he does not function effortlessly, as evidenced by his continual second-guessing of his motives in his interior monologues. We see the tension between Robert Jordan's emotions and his sense of duty echoed in the tension between his guilt at killing peasants who happen to be soldiers in the Fascist army and his commitment to the Republican cause. Hemingway sets up Robert Jordan's unwillingness to commit fully to Maria alongside the other tensions so that they reinforce one another, heightening the effect and adding to the drama of the resolution.

Throughout the novel, we see the characters routinely make decisions about the value of human life that they would consider dishonorable during peacetime. If the more practical Robert Jordan and Pilar failed to stop the more idealistic Primitivo, Primitivo would go to support El Sordo upon realizing that El Sordo's hilltop has been attacked. Yet, admirable as Primitivo's bravery might seem, it would be the wrong choice for him to go—for he would be killed immediately, which would endanger not only the lives of the *guerrilleros* but also the bridge operation and the larger Republican offensive it serves. Similarly, Robert Jordan avoids thinking about any of the people he has killed, especially about the fact that the Fascist cavalryman that he kills has a sister and a fiancée. In order to cope, Robert Jordan decides that, during wartime, it is unproductive to dwell on the morality of one's actions. His statement that one has to "put many things in abeyance to win a war" highlights the wartime necessity of believing in the idea that the ends justify the means.

Hemingway's frequent use of animal imagery links the human action of the novel to the natural world—a connection the characters themselves sometimes recognize. Hemingway often uses this animal imagery in symbolic fashion. The hares that Rafael catches mating in the snow, for example, recall Robert Jordan and Maria, both in their outdoor coupling and in Robert Jordan's nickname for Maria, "Rabbit." The fact that the hares die casts an ominous tone and foreshadows Robert Jordan and Maria's eventual separation, their entrapment by forces larger than themselves. In addition to the links Hemingway himself draws between the human and natural worlds, the characters of the novel make similar links on their own. For example, Robert Jordan compares the planes flying overhead to "sharks," and Rafael speaks of an exploding train as a "great wounded animal." These comparisons imply that the natural world is the world that the *guerrilleros* understand best. This alignment of the *guerrilleros* with the natural world and the Fascist side with the modern, industrialized world runs throughout *For Whom the Bell Tolls*. The comparison of the Fascist planes to sharks casts the Fascists as predators who threaten the natural world with their military and industrial power, which will eventually render the natural lifestyle of the *guerrilleros* obsolete.

Chapters Twenty-seven–Twenty-nine

Summary: Chapter Twenty-seven

> *"Pasionaria says 'Better to die on thy—'" Joaquín was saying to himself as the drone came nearer them. Then he shifted suddenly into "Hail Mary, full of grace, the Lord is with thee...."*
>
> *(See* Quotations, *p. 62)*

El Sordo and his small group of fighters defend their hill. El Sordo, who has received three wounds already, also must shoot his wounded horse. The zealous teenage fighter Joaquín invokes a slogan of the Communist party, but other fighters deflate his enthusiasm, claiming that three major leaders of the Communist Party all have sons who are not fighting in the war. El Sordo expects that planes will soon come and bomb the hill.

Just before three o'clock in the afternoon, the Fascists attacking El Sordo's hill wait for the planes to arrive. Captain Moro, sure that all the guerrillas are dead, wants his Lieutenant Paco Berrendo and other men to advance, but they are afraid. When Captain Moro finally comes out of cover, El Sordo shoots him dead. The planes arrive and bomb the hill, killing all the guerrillas except Joaquín. Lieutenant Berrendo then shoots Joaquín and orders the beheading of all the guerrilla fighters. However, he does not stay to watch his orders carried out.

Summary: Chapter Twenty-eight

After the planes leave, the men at Pablo's camp halfheartedly eat the stewed hare with mushrooms that Pilar has prepared for them. Later, Primitivo and Robert Jordan see a cavalry column riding along the road with an officer at the head. The officer is Lieutenant Berrendo, who feels remorse for having cut off the heads of the *guerrilleros'* corpses. He remembers his dead friend Julián and begins to pray.

Anselmo, returning from La Granja, also sees Lieutenant Berrendo's column ride past. He passes by El Sordo's hill and sees that the corpses have been beheaded. Horrified, he prays for the first time since the start of the Republican movement. The prayer makes him feel better. When Anselmo arrives at the camp, Fernando tells him that Pablo has also already seen the corpses and told everyone about what happened to El Sordo.

Summary: Chapter Twenty-nine

Anselmo reports to Robert Jordan what kind of preparations the Fascists have been making. After consulting with Anselmo, Robert Jordan sends Andrés across enemy lines to headquarters in Navacerrada with a letter to General Golz. In the letter, Robert Jordan recommends that both the bridge-blowing operation and the larger offensive be canceled. He explains the confusing bureaucracy of the military machine to Anselmo. As Robert Jordan writes the letter to General Golz, Pablo compliments him for his presence of mind and good judgment.

Analysis: Chapters Twenty-seven–Twenty-nine

Joaquín's and Anselmo's returns to religion at crucial moments of terror and solitude reveal the spiritual emptiness of the Republican side. The Republican government made religion illegal when it assumed power six years before the action portrayed in *For Whom the Bell Tolls*. Hemingway criticizes the Republican leaders' failure to provide the Spanish people with any spiritual solace to fill the void left by the banning of religion. Despite their beliefs in the Republic and official repudiation of organized religion, both Joaquín and Anselmo discover that their unquestioning faith in the Republic is unsatisfying. Although Joaquín initially faces the Fascists' attack by reciting Communist slogans, he turns to the prayers of his childhood when the bombing begins because he realizes that the Communist rhetoric is empty. Similarly, Anselmo turns to prayer for solace when he discovers El Sordo's men beheaded. Hemingway uses religion to highlight an important failure in the Republican leadership, a failure that he sees as a form of betrayal of the Spanish people.

Hemingway portrays the Fascist Lieutenant Berrendo as a sympathetic character, which complicates our tendency to identify the Republican side as good and the Fascist side as bad. Lieutenant Berrendo's grief at losing his friend Julián humanizes him. We identify with and admire him for his disapproval of his pompous, incompetent captain. Berrendo is introspective even in his somewhat half-hearted remorse in ordering the beheading of El Sordo and his men. In this light, the battle on El Sordo's hilltop is a struggle not between impersonal opposing armies but between sympathetic human beings like Lieutenant Berrendo and El Sordo. Hemingway's description of the battle calls into question the reasons the war is fought in the first place and poignantly renders the deaths of the men useless.

Our sympathy with Lieutenant Berrendo becomes more complete during his interior monologues, which are startlingly reminiscent of Robert Jordan's. Like Robert Jordan, Berrendo questions his motivations and interpretations of the difficult decisions that he must make. The main difference is that Robert Jordan is both more competent and more cynical; he has progressed beyond trite phrases like Lieutenant Berrendo's "What a bad thing war is." Nevertheless, Hemingway's complicated presentation of war as a conflict between two imperfect sides consisting of imperfect yet sympathetic individuals is another form of innocence destroyed by the war—the innocence of readers who expect their sympathies to be guided by easy moral choices.

Chapters Thirty–Thirty-three

Summary: Chapter Thirty

Robert Jordan thinks to himself as he walks back from Primitivo's post. He struggles with the conflict between wanting to follow orders and believing that the orders are useless. He remembers his family. His mother bullied his weak father, who finally committed suicide with the same rifle that his own father had used in the American Civil War.

As Robert Jordan imagines a tremendous success in the next day's offensive, he realizes that the bridge-blowing operation won't be called off because those making the decision won't be able to help themselves from imagining the same success he imagines. The certainty calms him down.

Summary: Chapter Thirty-one

Robert Jordan and Maria lie in his sleeping bag together. Maria says that she is sore, so they decide not to have intercourse, although Robert Jordan privately thinks that this bad luck the night before blowing up the bridge is a bad sign. Maria offers to bring him to orgasm some other way, but he declines.

Robert Jordan says that he'd rather not talk about the present, so they imagine their future life in Madrid. Their reverie is briefly interrupted when Maria reveals that Pilar predicted that they would all die tomorrow. Pilar's indiscretion angers Robert Jordan.

Maria then talks about the day she was captured. The Fascists shot both of her parents against a wall. Her father was the mayor of their town, and his last words were for the Republic. Maria's mother's last words were about Maria's father. The Fascists cut off Maria's hair, gagged her with her own braids, drew the letters UHP (*Unión de Hermanos Proletarios*, a Communist association) on her forehead, and then took her into her father's office and took turns raping her. Maria wants Robert Jordan to know that she struggled the whole time, and that Pilar suggested that the violent incident may have left Maria infertile. Robert Jordan promises that they will get married. After she falls asleep, he calms his anger by telling himself that both sides have committed atrocities in the war. He wishes that they could have made love and admires Maria's mother's last words.

Summary: Chapter Thirty-two

In Madrid, Robert Jordan's friend Karkov arrives at his apartments at the Hotel Gaylord and greets his wife and German-speaking mistress. Karkov finds out that the German commander has been telling everyone about the next day's offensive. A puffy-eyed journalist for the Russian newspaper *Izvestia* informs Karkov that La Pasionaria (a Communist orator whose real name is Dolores) has brought news that the Fascists have been bombing their own troops near Segovia.

In conversation with a Hungarian general, Karkov expresses annoyance with both the German commander's and the journalist's indiscretions. Karkov is also concerned about Robert Jordan, whom he knows to be working for General Golz near Segovia. The Hungarian general expects that Robert Jordan will send a report on the bombing but does not want to go to headquarters to check for a report because he does not feel welcome there. Karkov goes to sleep, planning to wake up at two in the morning to join Golz for the offensive.

Summary: Chapter Thirty-three

At two in the morning, Pilar wakes Robert Jordan up and tells him that Pablo has fled the camp with some of the dynamite they were to use to blow up the bridge. Although Robert Jordan is angry at Pilar, who was supposed to be guarding the dynamite, he curbs his anger because she feels terrible. Pilar feels that she has betrayed not only her promise to Robert Jordan but also the Republic. Robert Jordan goes back to sleep, planning to wake up at four.

Analysis: Chapters Thirty–Thirty-three

Robert Jordan's extended memories of his father and grandfather show how the characters in *For Whom the Bell Tolls* must work actively to overcome their pasts. Robert Jordan is saddened that he never knew his grandfather, who was an admired hero in the American Civil War, and is embarrassed by the weakness of his father, who committed suicide. Ultimately, though, Robert Jordan does not dwell on either. He forces himself to call his father a "coward" despite the fact that doing so is unpleasant. He constantly works through his memories in order to rob them of their power. Similarly, by engaging in sexual activity with someone she loves, Maria confronts her rape until it "is all gone." Although it may seem odd to contemporary readers to read about characters who suppress memories as a way of coping with them, this ability to leave the past in the past and live fully in the present is one of the features of Hemingway's code of values. As we have seen earlier, Robert Jordan avoids thinking about the people he has killed, for guilt is not productive during wartime. Only by actively suppressing unpleasant memories from the past are Hemingway's code heroes able to cope with the unpleasant realities of the present.

Hemingway frequently describes Maria with natural, earthy imagery, showing that she represents the pull of nature in Robert Jordan's life. Throughout the novel, Hemingway paints Maria in earth tones, with hair "the golden brown of a grain field," "breasts like small hills," and a belly button like a well on a plain. These images demonstrate Maria's strong, organic connection to the earth. Indeed, it is during his sexual experience with Maria that the earth moves for Robert Jordan. One critic suggests that the earthy imagery indicates that Maria is the Spanish land, raped and pillaged by warring forces beyond her comprehension, yet always loving and soothing. Robert Jordan's communion with Maria, then, is also a communion with his chosen country. His progression from isolation at the beginning of the novel toward a full union with Maria by the end is a journey toward a fertile, earthy affirmation of life, guided by instinct rather than reason.

In the chapter set at the Hotel Gaylord, Hemingway criticizes the Republican leadership, whose apathy, incompetence, and factionalism bears a large part of the blame for the Republicans' eventual defeat. Accordingly, Hemingway portrays his Republican high society characters as uncaring, gossipy, self-indulgent, and stupid. The setting in a fancy hotel contrasts starkly with the cave where Robert Jordan and the *guerrilleros* sleep, implying that Republican leaders don't care about the conditions of their own people. We also see this lack of involvement in the Hungarian general: he says he could go to headquarters and find out whether Robert Jordan has sent word, but he doesn't like headquarters and consequently won't go. The general's apathy seals the fate of Robert Jordan as well as countless others. Even those characters who are not apathetic care about the wrong things. The dramatic irony in La Pasionaria's story is that the Fascists actually bombed El Sordo, not their own troops. But the puffy-eyed journalist focuses on La Pasionaria's theatricality rather than on the misinterpreted content of the story. In the end, the chapter leaves us with the impression that the *guerrilleros* are the only ones on the Republican side who truly know what is taking place in the war, while the Republican leadership is frustratingly out of touch. We find ourselves asking the same question Hemingway and Robert Jordan ask: "Have there ever been people more betrayed by their own leaders?"

Chapters Thirty-four–Thirty-nine

Summary: Chapter Thirty-four

Andrés rides through the night to deliver Robert Jordan's dispatch to General Golz. He thinks about his feeling of relief when Robert Jordan asked him to deliver his message—relief because killing thrills Andrés in a way that embarrasses him. He remembers having the same feeling of exhilaration and embarrassment on his town's annual bull-baiting day, in which, by tradition, he was expected to bite the bull by the ear. He also remembers feeling the same sense of relief if the bull-baiting ever was canceled. Andrés arrives at a checkpoint.

Summary: Chapter Thirty-Five

Robert Jordan lies next to Maria, seething with anger at Pablo and reproaching himself for letting Pablo steal from his packs. He forces himself to let go of his anger. Calm, he thinks about how to blow up the bridge without enough people, horses, or weapons, and now without the mechanism for properly detonating the dynamite. Robert Jordan whispers to the sleeping Maria that they can still finish the mission. They will all be killed, he thinks, but they will complete their task. He tells Maria that a good night's sleep will be her wedding present.

Summary: Chapter Thirty-Six

At the checkpoint, the guards challenge, insult, and threaten to shoot Andrés. After much wrangling, Andrés finally convinces them that his mission is legitimate. One of the guards takes Andrés's gun and escorts him down the hill.

Summary: Chapter Thirty-Seven

Robert Jordan and Maria lie in bed just before three in the morning. He licks her ear, and she wakes up. They make love, and once again they experience a simultaneous orgasm and feel the earth move. Maria calls this state "*la gloria.*" They talk about how lucky they are to have found each other. Robert Jordan thinks that these people—Maria, Pilar, Anselmo, Agustín—are his family, and that he has been here at the fort his whole life. He thinks about how much he has learned.

Summary: Chapter Thirty-Eight

Before dawn, the guerrilla fighters eat breakfast and nervously prepare for the attack later that day. Robert Jordan plans to use hand grenades to make up for the stolen explosives. He thinks that they have too few men and that the attack will fail. He struggles to overcome his anger at Pablo. Pilar tells Robert Jordan that she cares about him very much and that he should forget about how troubled she seemed after reading his palm.

Pablo suddenly returns to the camp. He has thrown the explosives he stole into the river but has brought five men with their horses from neighboring guerrilla bands. He explains that he left in a moment of weakness and that he felt great loneliness after he threw the explosives in the river. Although Pilar compares Pablo to Judas Iscariot (the biblical apostle who betrays Jesus), both Pilar and Robert Jordan are relieved that Pablo has returned.

Summary: Chapter Thirty-nine

Having packed up the camp, the guerrilla fighters begin to take their positions for the bridge operation. Though Robert Jordan doesn't believe in luck, he takes Pablo's return as a positive sign. He engages in brief conversations with Pablo and Maria. Pilar recognizes and greets two of the five men that have come with Pablo.

Analysis: Chapters Thirty-four–Thirty-nine

Robert Jordan's competent behavior under difficult circumstances in this section fits him in to a line of Hemingway protagonists who exhibit what Hemingway calls "grace under pressure." Nowhere more than here does Robert Jordan display this virtue of the code hero. With Pablo gone and the explosives stolen, Robert Jordan manages to control his anger and apply himself to solving the new, more difficult problem of destroying the bridge with less manpower and fewer explosives. Always supremely pragmatic, Robert Jordan neither dwells on the past nor fears the future but instead concentrates on the present situation. This focus on the present allows him to savor fully the physical pleasures that fate grants him—the smell of pine trees, the taste of absinthe, sex with Maria. It also enables him not to fear death, which is the code hero's true antagonist. Ultimately, Robert Jordan's level-headedness is the only force that holds the *guerrilleros* together in the face of daunting odds.

The words "now" and "one," which dominate Robert Jordan's consciousness during his lovemaking with Maria on the morning of the attack, point to his appreciation of life in the present and the wholeness of their communion with each other. The present "now" is the only time that he has with Maria, for they barely have a past, and the future is uncertain. Robert Jordan frequently thinks that he is living his whole, full life in the seventy hours portrayed in *For Whom the Bell Tolls*. When focusing on the present, Robert Jordan sees the "now" as representing "now and before and always." He stops thinking about the future and the probability of his death—in a sense, he transcends death and becomes temporarily immortal. This immortality becomes possible through Maria's idea that Robert Jordan and she are "one" person. And indeed, the word "one" pervades their conversation after sex. Robert Jordan and Maria's communion is complete, blessed and sealed by the natural forces that move the earth. Robert Jordan's new feelings—his growing thoughts about the concept of "now" and his feeling of being "one" with Maria—are rather non-scientific and non-rational. As the novel draws to its close, we see that Robert Jordan gradually moves toward accepting and embracing Pilar's brand of mysticism and supernatural wisdom.

Hemingway's description of Andrés baiting the bull emphasizes the connection between death and sex in the novel. Andrés remembers how "he lay on the hot, dusty, bristly, tossing slope of the muscle, the ear clenched tight in his teeth, and drove his knife again and again and again into the swelling, tossing bulge of the neck that was now spouting hot on his fist." The strong sexual overtones are unmistakable, especially in "spouting hot" and "again and again and again," which echoes the rhythm of the passages about Robert Jordan and Maria's lovemaking. The high that Andrés experiences after bull-baiting is a sexual one, which explains both its addictiveness and the sense of shame that accompanies it. Importantly, the realm in which Andrés gained his experience in killing—bull-baiting—was a relatively controlled environment. The experience of killing under his belt, Andrés knows how to recognize the urge to kill and consequently how to control it. But Pablo's first experience with killing was the massacre of the Fascists in his town. He never had the opportunity to face his cruelty in a controlled environment and never learned to control his passions, which makes him dangerous. In connecting bloodlust and sexual lust in this manner throughout the novel, Hemingway implies that the desire for violence is as common a sensation as sexual desire—a bold statement about human nature.

Chapters Forty–Forty-two

Summary: Chapter Forty

The Republican military bureaucracy slows Andrés's progress considerably. Andrés meets Captain Gomez, the battalion commander of the company Andrés encountered at the checkpoint. Gomez escorts Andrés to the brigade command office in his motorcycle. They pass war-ravaged trees on their way.

At the brigade command office, Gomez requests to speak to a superior, Lieutenant-Colonel Miranda. An apathetic subordinate officer says that Miranda is sleeping and refuses to wake him up until Gomez threatens the officer with a gun. A short time later, Miranda walks into the room and orders his subordinate officer to type up a letter of safe conduct for Andrés. Miranda orders Gomez to escort Andrés to General Golz's headquarters.

Summary: Chapter Forty-one

The guerrilla fighters reach the place where they plan to leave their horses. The horses are to be Maria's responsibility during the operation. Robert Jordan once again asks Pilar whether she understands what she is supposed to do, which greatly irritates her. He says goodbye to Pablo and is surprised by Pablo's firm handshake. Robert Jordan thinks that perhaps all allies, like he and Pablo, hate each other deep down.

As Robert Jordan awkwardly says goodbye to Maria, he has a sense of déjà vu and feels very young. He is reminded of going away to school for the first time. He first felt very young and scared, but then, embarrassed by his father's tearful good-bye, felt very old.

Robert Jordan, Anselmo, and Agustín separate from the rest of the group and head toward the bridge. Robert Jordan helps Agustín set up the machine gun and advises Anselmo about how to shoot one of the sentries. Robert Jordan takes his position and waits for daylight.

Summary: Chapter Forty-two

A truck accident delays Andrés and Gomez on their journey to General Golz's headquarters. When they finally arrive, Gomez recognizes André Marty, a well-known military advisor, and asks him for help in locating General Golz. But Marty, who has become somewhat paranoid during the war, is suspicious and orders Andrés and Gomez arrested as Fascists.

The narrator interjects to tell us that Marty, supported by the flawed wartime bureaucratic system, has launched a number of ill-advised combat missions, much to General Golz's dismay. The narrator adds, however, that the military machine is so poorly organized that it is unlikely that the Republican offensive could have been stopped even if Andrés had not been delayed.

Robert Jordan's friend Karkov finds out about the arrest, confronts Marty, and uses his power as a well-connected journalist to send Andrés and Gomez to headquarters. At last, Robert Jordan's dispatch reaches Duval, Golz's chief of staff. Duval considers calling off the Republican offensive even though he doesn't officially have the authority to do so, but ultimately he decides against it because he doesn't know how this offensive fits into the bigger picture of the war. By the time Golz sees the dispatch and learns that his attack will fail, it is too late and the bombing has already begun.

Analysis: Chapters Forty–Forty-two

Hemingway continues to criticize the Republican leadership, now turning his focus toward the inefficiency of their bureaucracy. He implies, in the chapters that chronicle Andrés's mission, that the eventual Republican defeat was at least partly the fault of the Republicans' poor organization. In the course of his quest, Andrés is delayed by apathy, suspicion, and personal vendetta—all of which are made possible by the inefficiency and corruption of the Republican military. Ironically, Andrés travels faster behind enemy lines than within Republican territory, where the Republican military organization hinders rather than helps its own cause. Lieutenant-Colonel Miranda is more committed to the bureaucratic system than to the cause that the system was designed to serve—an attitude that hinders Andrés under the guise of helping him. Above all, André Marty (a real historical figure who was the Political Commissar of the International Brigades, a coalition of foreign volunteers), comes across as stupid, paranoid, insecure, and corrupt. Because the influential Marty is in a position to do the most damage, he receives Hemingway's most scathing critique. But even the journalist Karkov, in many ways an admirable character, falls prey to political factionism. The conflict between Karkov and Marty seems to be as personal as it is political.

Just as the impersonal bureaucracy menaces Andrés's mission, it also menaces the simple, organic world of the *guerrilleros*. As the wartime bureaucratic structures take control of towns and cities, the local population is either swept up in the changes or left behind. Some alter their lives, while others, like much of the gypsy population, move in circles outside mainstream society. In either case, life close to nature becomes impossible, and the development of military bureaucracy heralds the end of an era. Like the Fascist planes, the military bureaucracy menaces both the Republic and the lifestyle of its citizens.

The two interweaving narratives of this section—Andrés's quest to deliver the message and Robert Jordan's quest to blow the bridge—mirror and reinforce each other. At approximately the same time in the night that Pablo's reappearance boosts Robert Jordan's cause (Chapter Thirty-eight), Karkov unexpectedly aids Andrés's mission (Chapter Forty-two). Furthermore, the pattern of events that take place during Andrés's mission in Chapter Forty-two—a halting struggle, temporary triumph, and final letdown—foreshadows the pattern of events that occur when Robert Jordan attempts to blow up the bridge in Chapter Forty-three. Hemingway structures these two sets of events to cycle, one after the other, for dramatic and atmospheric effect. By the time we read it, the story that unfolds in the final chapter has already been told.

Chapter Forty-three

Summary

> *He was completely integrated now and he took a good long look at everything.*
>
> (See Quotations, p. 63)

From his position on the ground, Robert Jordan watches the dawn, observes a squirrel, and smells the pine trees. He recognizes one of the sentries on the bridge from surveying the site earlier.

The bombing—the cue for blowing up the bridge—begins. Robert Jordan and Anselmo shoot the two sentries on the bridge and affix the dynamite to the near end of the bridge. As Robert Jordan goes to attach the dynamite to the far end, Pilar returns with her group. Eladio has been shot through the head and Fernando mortally wounded. At Fernando's request, Primitivo and Rafael leave Fernando with a rifle near the bridge.

Anselmo feels "one with" the world as he waits for Robert Jordan to finish the setup on the other side of the bridge. They detonate the dynamite just as a truck prepares to cross the bridge. Anselmo is killed by a flying block of steel. In the aftermath of the explosion, Robert Jordan feels angry, especially at Anselmo's death. Speaking to Pilar, he gradually lets go of his anger.

Meanwhile, Maria watches the horses. The animals sense her nervousness and become nervous themselves. Maria prays for Robert Jordan's safe return and is relieved when she hears Pilar shout that he is safe. Robert Jordan checks in with Agustín, who has been manning the machine gun. Pablo returns alone and says that his other men are dead. Agustín accuses Pablo of shooting the other men for their horses, and Pablo does not deny it.

The men return to Maria and the horses. Robert Jordan embraces her, realizing that, for the first time in his life, he has been able to hold onto his feelings for a woman during battle. They mount the horses, and Pablo prepares to lead them to the Gredos mountains. Robert Jordan mounts the horse of the cavalryman he killed the previous day. He rides last in the caravan, directly behind Maria.

As they cross the main road, a Fascist bullet hits Robert Jordan's horse, which tramples on Robert Jordan's left leg, breaking it. Realizing that he will have to stay behind, Robert Jordan talks to Pablo and tells him to use his head. Then Robert Jordan speaks to Maria, and tells her that although he must stay behind, when she leaves he will be with her. Agustín offers to shoot him out of mercy, but Robert Jordan refuses and asks him to take care of Maria.

Alone, Robert Jordan waits for the Fascists to come. He is sorry that he must die but grateful for how much he has learned and how much he has lived in the last three days. His leg begins to hurt, and he briefly contemplates suicide. He convinces himself to hold on until he can shoot some of the Fascists to buy the *guerrilleros* some getaway time.

As Robert Jordan begins to pass out, he finally sees the approaching Fascist cavalry patrol, led by Lieutenant Berrendo, the man who ordered the beheading of El Sordo's men. Feeling "completely integrated" into his world—the road, the sky, the pine needles—Robert Jordan takes aim, waits for Berrendo to ride closer, and feels his heart beat against the forest floor.

ANALYSIS

The final chapter of *For Whom the Bell Tolls* resolves the many tensions with which Robert Jordan struggles throughout the novel. We have seen Robert Jordan demonstrate a tension between intuition and skepticism. Although he frequently claims not to believe in signs and portents, he plays games with himself, identifying certain events as good or bad omens. In the final chapter of the novel, he acknowledges that the gypsies "see something. Or they feel something. Like a bird dog." It seems that he finally agrees with Pilar that the world is more mysterious than his cold reasoning can explain. Similarly, the tension between feeling and duty, which Hemingway portrays through Robert Jordan's rejection of Maria whenever he thinks about his mission, is resolved as Robert Jordan embraces Maria during battle. As women, Maria and Pilar are associated, both traditionally and in *For Whom the Bell Tolls*, with intuitive feeling— they are represented by the heart. Skepticism and work, traditionally the domain of men, are associated with thought, represented by the head. Over the course of the novel, Robert Jordan gradually integrates these forces of heart and head in order to become a complete person. The resolution culminates in Hemingway's description of Robert Jordan as "completely integrated." His tensions are resolved, the clamor of constant self-questioning in his mind ceases, and he is at finally at peace with his world.

Robert Jordan's physical position at the very end of the novel symbolizes his relationship with the land. He lies on the ground, literally embracing his beloved Spanish landscape. He loves the physical earth, especially the pine needles he has noticed and smelled from the opening of the novel. He loves the country, which he has worked to defend from what he sees as the Fascist menace. And he loves the land as a representation of the simpler, earthier, more traditional, intuitive, and natural lifestyle that the land supports—and that Pilar, as a superstitious female gypsy, embodies. Several times throughout the novel, Hemingway uses the image of Robert Jordan lying on the earth to highlight these associations. Literally and figuratively, Robert Jordan's heart beats with the earth.

Furthermore, Robert Jordan's position at the very end of the novel is almost identical to his position at the very beginning, which reveals the novel's circular structure and highlights how Robert Jordan has changed during the course of the story. The novel opens with Robert Jordan "[lying] flat on the brown, pine-needled floor of the forest" and closes with him feeling "his heart beating against the pine needle floor of the forest." The two phrases are almost identical, which implies that we can view the course of the novel as one cycle in Robert Jordan's life, one spin on the "wheel of human conflict" that Robert Jordan imagines after his second confrontation with Pablo. The new element at the end of the novel is Robert Jordan's beating heart, which he has figuratively discovered through his relationship with Maria and the *guerrilleros*. Hemingway describes the change in his protagonist as Robert Jordan greets Maria after blowing the bridge, saying, "He had never thought that you could know that there was a woman if there was battle." Unlike earlier instances in which he pushes Maria away when he is busy thinking about his mission, at the end of the novel, Robert Jordan is able to embrace Maria during the course of the battle. Hemingway encapsulates Robert Jordan's new ability to love while living through the image of the beating heart that closes the novel.

Important Quotations Explained

1. For him it was a dark passage which led to nowhere, then to nowhere, then again to nowhere, once again to nowhere, always and forever to nowhere . . .

This quotation from Chapter Thirteen describes Maria and Robert Jordan's lovemaking on their way back from visiting El Sordo. Hemingway's language in this passage strives to imitate the sexual act and re-create the structure of the experience for the reader. We can identify the repetitive rhythm of sexual intercourse: "[I]t was a dark passage which led to nowhere, then to nowhere, then again to nowhere, once again to nowhere . . ." The passage goes on to describe the climax: "up, up, up . . ." and the ejaculation: "and into nowhere, suddenly, scaldingly, holdingly . . . ." Finally, with "all nowhere gone and time absolutely still and they were both there, time having stopped and he felt the earth move out and away from under them," the jumble of words reorganizes itself back into grammatical clauses, mimicking the post-climactic regaining of the senses. This last phrase returns to the physical description that is typical of Robert Jordan's point of view throughout the novel. Here as often elsewhere throughout the novel, Hemingway's writing style mirrors Robert Jordan's psychological state. Just as, most of the time, the controlled, direct prose embodies Robert Jordan's clear, logical thinking, the confusion and loss of control over language in this passage reflects Robert Jordan's loss of physical and psychological control during sex.

2. . . . [Y]ou felt that you were taking part in a crusade. . . . [It] would be as difficult and embarrassing to speak about as a religious experience and yet it was authentic. . . . It gave you a part in something that you could believe in wholly and completely and in which you felt an absolute brotherhood with the others who were engaged in it.

This passage, from Chapter Eighteen, is an interior monologue in which Robert Jordan describes his earlier idealism about the war, which the realities of warfare have long since crushed. The passage gives us a glimpse of what may have caused Robert Jordan to leave his life and job in the states to volunteer to fight in a foreign war: he sought something to believe in "wholly and completely" and also sought communion, an "absolute brotherhood" with other people. But his disillusionment with the "bureaucracy and inefficiency and party strife" he sees in the Republican cause and its leaders foreshadows his current opinion that the leaders have "betrayed" their people. The religious vocabulary Hemingway uses, such as "crusade," "communion," "consecration," emphasizes the depth of Robert Jordan's feelings and suggests that, for many people, the Republican cause became a substitute religion. But Robert Jordan's use of religious language is accompanied by a touch of irony, since he immediately distances himself from using religious metaphors, which he characterizes as "embarrassing." This constant qualification of exactly what he means is typical of Robert Jordan's monologues.

Although Robert Jordan is jaded and cynical at the start of the novel, he comes to realize both his goals—his desire for something to believe in wholly and his desire for communion—by the end of the novel. Through his relationship with Maria, Robert Jordan finds love in which he can believe fully, love that he can integrate into his life. He also feels as if he has found family—an absolute brotherhood—with the *guerrilleros*: "I have been all my life in these hills. . . . Anselmo is my oldest friend. . . . Agustín . . . is my brother. . . . Maria is my true love and my wife. . . . She is also my sister . . . and my daughter."

3. We do it coldly but they do not, nor ever have. It is their extra sacrament.... They are the people of the Auto de Fé; the act of faith. Killing is something one must do, but ours are different from theirs.

After the *guerrilleros* hide from four passing Fascist cavalrymen in Chapter Twenty-three, Agustín reveals that the anxiety he experienced was caused not only by fear, but also by a thirst for the kill. In this passage, which comes directly afterward, Robert Jordan reflects on the particular nature of Spaniards. He believes that, as a race, they have an innate, pre-Christian, visceral desire to kill that has surfaced periodically throughout history. He references the Spanish Inquisition, the state-sponsored brutal persecution of Jews and other non-Catholics that was practiced in Spain from the Renaissance through the beginning of the nineteenth century. Robert Jordan ends by forcing himself to face up to the fact that he, too, has felt the urge and excitement of killing. In several instances throughout the novel, most notably in the language that he uses to describe Andrés's memories of bull-baiting in his hometown in Chapter Thirty-four, Hemingway draws parallels between the drive to kill and the desire for sex. Through this parallel, Hemingway establishes yet another connection between death and sex, a major motif in the novel.

4. "Pasionaria says 'Better to die on thy—'" Joaquín was saying to himself as the drone came nearer them. Then he shifted suddenly into "Hail Mary, full of grace, the Lord is with thee...."

This excerpt comes from Chapter Twenty-seven, El Sordo's last stand on his hill. The quotation, spoken by El Sordo's young companion Joaquín, starkly illustrates the inadequacies of the Republican government and its leadership in the war. The Republican government outlawed religion when it came to power six years earlier, and the teenage Joaquín came of age under its propaganda. He clings to Republican rhetoric throughout the attack on the hill, despite the laughter of his older and more cynical comrades. The Republicans' empty words prove to be cold comfort as Joaquín faces death. Hemingway views this empty rhetoric as a betrayal of the true needs of the Spanish peasants, who had grown up with religion and see it as a comfort. Indeed, as Joaquín faces death, he remembers his Catholic childhood—his beliefs before the Republicans outlawed religion—and prays to the Virgin Mary. Likewise, Anselmo turns to prayer as he beholds the beheaded Joaquín and his comrades not long after. Ultimately, although most of the protagonists of Hemingway's novels, including Robert Jordan, do not believe in God, Hemingway does not criticize the need to rely on religion for support.

5. He was completely integrated now and he took a good long look at everything. Then he looked up at the sky. There were big white clouds in it. He touched the palm of his hand against the pine needles where he lay and he touched the bark of the pine trunk that he lay behind.

This passage from the last chapter of the novel describes Robert Jordan at the moment when, wounded and alone, he realizes that he will be able to stay alive long enough to ambush the approaching Fascist cavalry, thereby buying the *guerrilleros* some time to escape. The passage, especially its first phrase, provides a climactic resolution of one of the novel's themes—Robert Jordan's continual struggle with himself to figure out his motives and his purpose. For the first time, he feels "completely integrated" with his world.

Having rejected Communism sometime before the start of the novel, Robert Jordan now embraces not some abstract idea of a brotherhood of men but the concrete human relationships he has forged with a specific group of *guerrilleros*. After long proclaiming that he does not believe in Pilar's signs and omens, he now accepts the possibility that "[the gypsies] see something. Or they feel something." Having spent much of the novel arguing with himself about abstractions, Robert Jordan is now at peace simply to appreciate and say goodbye to his physical surroundings with his concrete, physical senses.

The style of this passage is classic Hemingway. The phrase structures are the simplest possible—there are no commas. The sentence structure's only complexity, the tendency toward run-ons, gives the sentences a concrete, physical shape, like a flowing river. Also typical of Hemingway, the simplicity of the grammar hides the depth of feeling just below the surface: Robert Jordan touches the elements of his physical world, one by one, including the ever-present pines, in a gesture of final farewell. He knows he is about to die. Hemingway's language, with its deep feeling simmering below unadorned stoicism, is an echo of his hero.

Key Facts

FULL TITLE
For Whom the Bell Tolls

AUTHOR
Ernest Hemingway

TYPE OF WORK
Novel

GENRE
Tragedy; historical novel; war novel; love story

LANGUAGE
English sprinkled with Spanish words and phrases. Many sections, especially dialogue and interior monologue, are written as though they have been translated word-for-word from Spanish to English and retain the structure and cadence of the Spanish language.

TIME AND PLACE WRITTEN
March 1939–August 1940; Cuba, Key West, Wyoming, and Idaho

DATE OF FIRST PUBLICATION
October 21, 1940

PUBLISHER
Scribner's

NARRATOR
Anonymous third-person

POINT OF VIEW
The narrative is written in a detached, journalistic style that focuses on what the characters can see, hear, or smell. This description is often restricted to what Robert Jordan can see or hear. On a few occasions, most notably when introducing Pablo confiding to his horse and introducing Karkov's rescue of Andrés and Gomez in prison, the narrator comments on the unfolding action.

TONE

The tone is detached, solemn, and world-weary, especially when the narrative focuses on the perspective of Robert Jordan. There are recurring elements of dramatic irony (resulting from a discrepancy between what the characters know and what we as readers know) as characters fighting for the Republican side express optimism about the outcome of the war.

TENSE

Immediate past

SETTING (TIME)

Three days during the last week of May 1937, from Saturday afternoon to Tuesday midday; along with lengthy flashbacks to earlier episodes in the lives of different characters

SETTING (PLACE)

The Guadarrama mountain range in Spain; several flashbacks are set in a variety of places in Montana and throughout Spain

PROTAGONIST

Robert Jordan

MAJOR CONFLICT

As Robert Jordan and a small band of guerrilla fighters prepare to blow up a bridge with their limited resources and manpower, Robert Jordan and Pablo struggle for authority over the small band of guerrillas. Meanwhile, Robert Jordan and Maria cope with the pitfalls of falling in love during wartime.

RISING ACTION

Robert Jordan arrives at Pablo's camp, convinces the band members to help him fulfill his mission, and falls in love with Maria. He enlists the aid of nearby guerrilla leader El Sordo and clashes with Pablo. Snow falls. A band of Fascists attacks and slaughters El Sordo's men. Robert Jordan sends a dispatch to General Golz recommending that the Republican offensive be canceled. Pablo leaves the group and steals some of Robert Jordan's explosives.

CLIMAX

Pablo returns. Andrés delivers the dispatch too late, and the Republican offensive is not canceled. Robert Jordan and the guerrilla band blow up the bridge.

FALLING ACTION
Four people, including Robert Jordan, die or are fatally wounded. Pablo leads the others away, presumably to safety into the mountains.

THEMES
The loss of innocence in war; the value of human life; romantic love as salvation

MOTIFS
Rabbits and hares; the forest floor; signs and omens; suicide

SYMBOLS
Planes, tanks, and mortars; absinthe

FORESHADOWING
Robert Jordan's intuition that Pablo will be a danger to the bridge operation; Pilar's consternation at what she reads in Robert Jordan's palm; Agustín's warning to Robert Jordan to pay attention to his packs; Pilar's sense of foreboding as she watches Pablo after the men swear allegiance to her; Robert Jordan's worry about the tracks that El Sordo may have left when the snowstorm stops at night; Pilar's lengthy description of the smell of death

Study Questions & Essay Topics

Study Questions

1. *What does the novel's title mean? For whom does the bell toll? What bell?*

The phrase "for whom the bell tolls" comes from a short essay by the seventeenth-century British poet and religious writer John Donne. Hemingway excerpts a portion of the essay in the epigraph to his novel. In Donne's essay, "For whom does the bell toll?" is the imaginary question of a man who hears a funeral bell and asks about the person who has died. Donne's answer to this question is that, because none of us stands alone in the world, each human death affects all of us. Every funeral bell, therefore, "tolls for thee."

Thematically, the title *For Whom the Bell Tolls* emphasizes the importance of community and fellow-feeling—the values that initially incited Robert Jordan to leave his home country to fight a foreign war. Over time, however, Robert Jordan has seen these values become complicated by war-won cynicism and a lack of moral clarity in the corrupt and inept Republican leaders. Yet by the end of the novel, Robert Jordan learns to embrace these same values again, through the deep connections he establishes with the guerrilla fighters during his short time with them. Robert Jordan undertakes his very last living effort—to hold off the approaching Fascist cavalrymen—not because he subscribes to a particular ideology but because he wishes to aid the escape of a group of people whom he has grown to love.

More literally, the novel's title helps focus our interpretations of the scenes of brutality and killing that Hemingway portrays. The cruelty of the executions in Pablo's village left a moral scar on all those who witnessed or participated—Pilar, Pablo, and his mob. Likewise, Lieutenant Berrendo feels the effects not only of his friend's death but of the slaughter of El Sordo's men as well. Even Robert Jordan, who kills out of duty because he must, is unable to emerge unscathed. Hemingway neither judges the murderer not justifies the murder. Rather, the moral scars these murders leave are simply the necessary toll of a difficult war.

Politically, the title reflects Hemingway's stance, which, like Robert Jordan's, is anti-Fascist as opposed to pro-Communist. Like many western intellectuals at the time, Hemingway saw the Spanish Civil War as a symbolic struggle between authoritarianism and a more humanist and liberal alternative. In this light, the title underscores Hemingway's and his characters' sympathies in the war.

2. *The earth moves four times during the course of the novel—twice at moments of destruction and twice during Robert Jordan and Maria's lovemaking. What connects these different moments? What does the connection say about human nature according to Hemingway?*

Characters mention that the earth moves four times in *For Whom the Bell Tolls*—twice in moments connected with sex and twice in moments connected with violence and death. In addition to the two times the earth moves when Robert Jordan and Maria make love, Rafael recalls the moment during the train operation with Kashkin when the train exploded and "all of the earth seemed to rise in a great cloud of blackness." Likewise, when El Sordo's hill is bombed, Joaquín feels "the earth roll under his knees and then wave up to hit him in the face," then "roll under him with a roar," and finally "lurch under his belly." The similar imagery used in these four instances establishes a strong connection between sex and death.

This connection between sex and death runs both ways. On the one hand, orgasm is a moment of sensory obliteration akin to dying. Maria gives voice to this experience when she tells Robert Jordan that she "die[s] each time" they make love. The word "nowhere," which Hemingway uses repeatedly in describing Robert Jordan and Maria's sexual encounter after visiting El Sordo, recalls the nothingness against which the Hemingway code hero struggles. Hemingway further supports the connection between death and sex through several other metaphors. After seething over Pablo's betrayal, Robert Jordan feels his "red, black, blinding, killing anger" die, leaving him "as quiet . . . sharp, [and] cold-seeing as a man is after he has had sexual intercourse with a woman that he does not love."

In the opposite direction, several characters express the idea that the excitement of killing is akin to sexual pleasure. Rafael, Agustín, and Robert Jordan all admit to feeling excitement or thirst for the kill. After the mass executions of the Fascists that Pablo stages in his hometown, he tells Pilar that he does not want to have sex—the excitement of the kill has used up his sexual charge. The most vivid description of the connection between bloodlust and sexual lust comes in Andrés's memories of his bull-baiting days in Chapter Thirty-four. Andrés explicitly makes a connection between the euphoria of bull-baiting and the sensation aroused by killing people, and the language he uses to describe his struggle with the bull has undeniable sexual connotations.

Together, these parallels Hemingway draws between death and sex form a strong statement about human nature. But in recounting Andrés's and Robert Jordan's experiences, Hemingway offers a partial solution. Unlike Pablo, those who have had the opportunity to experience the thirst for blood in a controlled setting (like Andrés) can admit to these impulses and control them. Likewise, those who engage in enough introspection about their past violent deeds (like Robert Jordan) can notice the pattern and control their urges as well. The courage of the Hemingway code hero lies not in never experiencing fear, but in acting bravely despite the fear. Likewise, Hemingway implies that the full human being does not deny his bloodthirstiness but recognizes it and learns to live with honor and self-awareness.

3. *Robert Jordan, a foreigner in Spain, fights for a cause that he claims not to believe in. What does he believe in? What is he fighting for?*

Robert Jordan went to Spain voluntarily to fight because of his love of the Spanish land and its culture. He believed in pragmatism, "life, liberty, and the pursuit of happiness," which he thought would be impossible under a Fascist regime. Accordingly, he decided to fight against the Fascists, which meant he joins the Republican side. Initially, he experienced something like a religious faith in the Republican cause and felt an "absolute brotherhood" with his comrades-in-arms. As the war drags on, however, Robert Jordan realizes that he does not necessarily believe in or espouse the values of the Republicans—he realizes that he joined their side simply because they were the ones fighting against the Fascists. Because he fights for a side whose causes he does not necessarily support, Robert Jordan experiences a great deal of internal conflict. Disillusioned with the Republican cause and its leaders, he wonders what difference there is between the Fascist and Republican sides—if there is any difference at all.

The other major factor motivating Robert Jordan to fight is that his grandfather, whom he admires very much, fought in the American Civil War. Robert Jordan is embarrassed by his weak father, who committed suicide. In this light, fighting in a war provides a way for Robert Jordan to link himself to his grandfather. Like a number of other characters in the novel—such as Maria, who must work to overcome the traumatic memories of her rape—Robert Jordan must work actively to overcome the burden of his past. Only by enlisting in a war does he believe he can exorcise his embarrassment about his father's cowardice and match the bravery of his grandfather.

Suggested Essay Topics

1. *One of the most frequent criticisms of* for whom the bell tolls *is that Hemingway portrays Maria as too submissive and eager to please to be a believable character. Do you agree with this critique? What is the role of women in the novel?*

2. *The novel ends with Robert Jordan near death but still alive, feeling his "heart beating against the pine needle floor of the forest." What is the effect of this ending? How would the novel be different if it ended after his death? Which ending do you prefer?*

3. *Some have criticized Hemingway for romanticizing the Spanish peasantry, especially in passages such as "They are wonderful when they are good, he thought. There is no people like them when they are good, and when they go bad there is no people that is worse." Find at least one other passage that takes a similar tone. Do you agree with this criticism of Hemingway? If so, does his romantic portrayal of the peasants detract from the novel? If not, why not?*

4. *Robert Jordan projects a jaded, seen-it-all attitude throughout much of the novel, yet he also believes that "one thing done well ... may make all the difference." Is Robert Jordan a cynic or an idealist? Does his view of the world change during the course of the novel? How does his attitude differ from the narrator's?*

5. *Many characters in* for whom the bell tolls *remember or tell stories about their pasts. Pilar remembers her life with the toreador Finito and tells a long story about the brutal beginning of the war in Pablo's home town. Robert Jordan remembers his father and grandfather and meeting his friend Karkov in Madrid. Maria talks about the day the Fascists killed her parents and cut off her hair. Andrés remembers baiting bulls in his village. In a novel in which the action happens over a scant three days, what is the role of the past? How does it affect the present?*

Review & Resources

Quiz

1. What is Robert Jordan's nickname for Maria?

    A. Squirrel
    B. Rabbit
    C. Mouse
    D. Dove

2. Why does Maria have short hair?

    A. Fascists cut it when they pillaged her town
    B. Anarchists cut it while she was in prison
    C. Pilar cut it because short hair was more practical
    D. A hairdresser in Valladolid cut it because Maria wanted to look like Greta Garbo

3. Why does Rafael leave his post guarding the camp?

    A. He takes a nap on the pine needles of the forest floor
    B. He grows bored and takes a walk
    C. He leaves to trap two hares
    D. He has to hide from low-flying enemy planes

4. How did Pilar's relationship with the toreador Finito end?

    A. Finito left Pilar for Zulma, who was much less ugly than Pilar
    B. Finito died as a result of complications from injuries in a bullfight
    C. Finito was executed by the Fascists in his village
    D. Pilar left Finito for Pablo

5. Which of the following characters does not mention Maria's physical beauty at some point during the novel?

   A. Robert Jordan
   B. Agustín
   C. Pilar
   D. Pablo

6. How do the guerrilla fighters store their wine?

   A. In hollowed-out animal skins
   B. In barrels made from pine tree trunks
   C. In wine bottles
   D. In large leather flasks

7. What is Andrés's brother's name?

   A. Fernando
   B. Primitivo
   C. Eladio
   D. Pilar

8. What does Maria say that prompts Robert Jordan to tell her that he loves her?

   A. That she loves him
   B. That she is pregnant with his baby
   C. That she needs to hear him say it more often
   D. That she should not sleep with him if he does not love her

9. To whom does Pablo whisper affectionately on the night that Robert Jordan arrives at the guerrilla camp?

   A. Maria
   B. Pilar
   C. His horse
   D. Robert Jordan

10. Which members of the guerrilla camp are at least partly of gypsy descent?

    A. Rafael and Pilar
    B. Maria and Pilar
    C. Anselmo and Maria
    D. Pilar and Eladio

11. Approximately how many days do the events of the novel span?

    A. Two
    B. Three
    C. Five
    D. Eight

12. Which characters are referred to as "old"?

    A. Anselmo
    B. Anselmo and Primitivo
    C. Anselmo and Fernando
    D. Anselmo, Primitivo, and Fernando

13. Which member of the guerrilla band stays at his observation post throughout the snowstorm?

    A. Rafael
    B. El Sordo
    C. Andrés
    D. Anselmo

14. How did Kashkin die?

    A. He killed himself
    B. Robert Jordan shot him
    C. Fascists executed him
    D. He was put to death in the Stalinist purges

15. Which of the following characters fights on the Fascist side?

    A. Robert Jordan
    B. Rogelio Gomez
    C. Paco Berrendo
    D. André Marty

16. Who is killed or severely wounded by the explosion at the bridge?

    A. Robert Jordan
    B. Fernando
    C. Anselmo
    D. No one

17. What is *la gloria*?

    A. The term Andrés uses to describe the excitement he feels when baiting a bull
    B. The term Pilar uses to describe the trance she enters when she reads palms
    C. The term Robert Jordan uses to describe being integrated with the world
    D. The term Maria uses to describe a particular sexual experience

18. Who, to our knowledge, does not pray during the time span of the novel?

    A. Joaquín
    B. Anselmo
    C. Maria
    D. Robert Jordan

19. What does Robert Jordan compare to a merry-go-round?

    A. The cycle of his lovemaking with Maria
    B. The circle of trust between him and Anselmo
    C. The cycle of confrontations between him and Pablo
    D. The cycle of his life at the guerrilla camp

20. Who warns Robert Jordan to take Maria's love seriously?

    A. Agustín
    B. Fernando
    C. Pilar
    D. Primitivo

21. What is Robert Jordan's theory about why El Sordo's camp was attacked?

    A. Pablo betrayed the Republican cause and told the Fascists where they might find El Sordo
    B. El Sordo shot a Fascist cavalryman, and the Fascists followed the tracks that the cavalryman's horse made to El Sordo's camp
    C. Because the snow stopped falling earlier than expected, the Fascists were able to follow the tracks that El Sordo's men left while gathering horses
    D. The Fascist planes spotted El Sordo's camp from above

22. Why does Anselmo no longer pray if he says he misses it so much?

    A. His traumatic wartime experiences have made him an avowed atheist
    B. He no longer believes in God after hearing of the atrocities of the Holocaust
    C. Scientific discoveries have convinced him that God does not exist
    D. The Republican leadership outlawed religion

23. What was Robert Jordan's occupation in America?

    A. Teacher
    B. Journalist
    C. Lawyer
    D. Architect

24. During which war does the novel take place?

    A. Spanish-American War
    B. Spanish Civil War
    C. World War I
    D. World War II

25. What happens at the very end of the novel?
    A. The approaching lieutenant kills Robert Jordan
    B. Robert Jordan kills the approaching lieutenant
    C. Robert Jordan waits to shoot the approaching lieutenant
    D. Robert Jordan passes out

ANSWER KEY:
1: B; 2: A; 3: C; 4: B; 5 D; 6: A; 7: B; 8: D; 9: C; 10: A; 11: B; 12: B; 13: D; 14: B; 15: C; 16: C; 17: D; 18: D; 19: C; 20: A; 21: C; 22: D; 23: A; 24: B; 25: C

Suggestions for Further Reading

BAKER, CARLOS. *Ernest Hemingway: A Life Story*. New York: Charles Scribner's Sons, 1969.

———. "The Spanish Tragedy." In *Ernest Hemingway: The Writer as Artist*. Princeton, New Jersey: Princeton University Press, 1963.

BEACH, JOSEPH WARREN. "Style in *For Whom the Bell Tolls*." In *Ernest Hemingway: A Critique of Four Major Novels*. Ed. Carlos Baker. New York: Scribner, 1962.

HEMINGWAY, ERNEST. *The Sun Also Rises*. New York: Charles Scribner's Sons, 1926.

———. *A Farewell to Arms*. New York: Charles Scribner's Sons, 1929.

JOSEPHS, ALLEN. *For Whom the Bell Tolls: Ernest Hemingway's Undiscovered Country*. New York: Twayne Publishers, 1994.

———. "Hemingway's Poor Spanish: Chauvinism and Loss of Credibility in *For Whom the Bell Tolls*." In *Hemingway: A Revaluation*. Edited by Donald R. Noble. Troy, New York: Whitston, 1983.

SANDERSON, RENA, ed. *Blowing the Bridge: Essays on Hemingway and For Whom the Bell Tolls*. New York: Greenwood Press, 1992.

STANTON, EDWARD F. *Hemingway in Spain: A Pursuit*. Seattle: University of Washington Press, 1989.

THOMAS, HUGH. *The Spanish Civil War*. New York: Harper & Row, 1977.

SparkNotes Literature Guides

1984
The Adventures of
  Huckleberry Finn
The Aeneid
All Quiet on the
  Western Front
And Then There Were
  None
Angela's Ashes
Animal Farm
Anna Karenina
Anne of Green Gables
Anthem
Antony and Cleopatra
As I Lay Dying
As You Like It
Atlas Shrugged
The Awakening
The Autobiography of
  Malcolm X
The Bean Trees
The Bell Jar
Beloved
Beowulf
Billy Budd
Black Boy
Bless Me, Ultima
The Bluest Eye
Brave New World
The Brothers
  Karamazov
The Call of the Wild
Candide
The Canterbury Tales
Catch-22
The Catcher in the Rye
The Chocolate War
The Chosen
Cold Mountain
Cold Sassy Tree
The Color Purple
The Count of Monte
  Cristo
Crime and Punishment
The Crucible
Cry, the Beloved
  Country
Cyrano de Bergerac
David Copperfield
Death of a Salesman
The Death of Socrates

The Diary of a Young
  Girl
A Doll's House
Don Quixote
Dr. Faustus
Dr. Jekyll and Mr. Hyde
Dracula
Dune
Edith Hamilton's
  Mythology
Emma
Ethan Frome
Fahrenheit 451
Fallen Angels
A Farewell to Arms
Farewell to Manzanar
Flowers for Algernon
For Whom the Bell
  Tolls
The Fountainhead
Frankenstein
The Giver
The Glass Menagerie
Gone With the Wind
The Good Earth
The Grapes of Wrath
Great Expectations
The Great Gatsby
Grendel
Gulliver's Travels
Hamlet
The Handmaid's Tale
Hard Times
Harry Potter and the
  Sorcerer's Stone
Heart of Darkness
Henry IV, Part I
Henry V
Hiroshima
The Hobbit
The House of Seven
  Gables
I Know Why the Caged
  Bird Sings
The Iliad
Inferno
Inherit the Wind
Invisible Man
Jane Eyre
Johnny Tremain
The Joy Luck Club

Julius Caesar
The Jungle
The Killer Angels
King Lear
The Last of the
  Mohicans
Les Miserables
A Lesson Before Dying
The Little Prince
Little Women
Lord of the Flies
The Lord of the Rings
Macbeth
Madame Bovary
A Man for All Seasons
The Mayor of
  Casterbridge
The Merchant of Venice
A Midsummer Night's
  Dream
Moby Dick
Much Ado About
  Nothing
My Antonia
Narrative of the Life of
  Frederick Douglass
Native Son
The New Testament
Nicomachean Ethics
Night
Notes from
  Underground
The Odyssey
The Oedipus Plays
Of Mice and Men
The Old Man and the
  Sea
The Old Testament
Oliver Twist
The Once and Future
  King
One Day in the Life of
  Ivan Denisovich
One Flew Over the
  Cuckoo's Nest
One Hundred Years of
  Solitude
Othello
Our Town
The Outsiders
Paradise Lost

A Passage to India
The Pearl
The Picture of Dorian
  Gray
Poe's Short Stories
A Portrait of the Artist
  as a Young Man
Pride and Prejudice
The Prince
A Raisin in the Sun
The Red Badge of
  Courage
The Republic
Richard III
Robinson Crusoe
Romeo and Juliet
The Scarlet Letter
A Separate Peace
Silas Marner
Sir Gawain and the
  Green Knight
Slaughterhouse-Five
Snow Falling on Cedars
Song of Solomon
The Sound and the Fury
Steppenwolf
The Stranger
Streetcar Named
  Desire
The Sun Also Rises
A Tale of Two Cities
The Taming of the
  Shrew
The Tempest
Tess of the d'Ubervilles
Their Eyes Were
  Watching God
Things Fall Apart
The Things They
  Carried
To Kill a Mockingbird
To the Lighthouse
Tom Sawyer
Treasure Island
Twelfth Night
Ulysses
Uncle Tom's Cabin
Walden
War and Peace
Wuthering Heights
A Yellow Raft in Blue
  Water